POKING HOLES

STORIES

JUAN VALENCIA

ISBN: 9798356047848

Cover art and design by Indrid Cruel
Please, visit him on Instagram at:
@howlingheartsbookclub
Support this amazing artist!

For all of my beautiful visions.

TABLE OF CONTENTS

PART 1: HOLES

POKING HOLES

I love poking holes in my boy. I love the feeling of his feet on the steps leading up to my door, like I can feel them on me, like a soft pitter-pattering across the hairs on my arm with the tips of his fingers. I open the door and ask if he's mine, and he says yes with his empty button eyes staring back at me, trying to make my shape out in the dark. A baseball cap then falls on my dusty brown sofa, then his thick jacket undrapes from his thin shoulders, bones poking out even through his jersey. The needle is warm in my grip the entire time.

"Sit down," I mumble, startled a bit by my own voice, which I don't hear very often, but he's already sitting, going through this like it's a routine, and I don't like that per se, but I let him do as he wishes. I let him get comfortable, and I try to imagine that even in the freedom of his movements, even in the way he lounges back on the sofa, he's in the grip of this house, gelled up in its shut airs, the shelter of its walls another part of my tight grasp—a grasp that I always want to have on him. Feet wrapped in dirty sneakers land on my coffee table, and he asks for a cigarette, and I lie and tell him I've run out.

"You wanna do it right now?" he asks, straight to the point, the growing confidence in his lowered inflection leaving me cold, his words dropping with heavy thuds as I stare into his small, roach-colored eyes.

I hold back the urge to *really* go at him just then, to poke a hole so big through him, it might even overtake his entire frame. I hate the new lowness of his voice, how it *drools* out, penetrating the ear so thick and suffocating. I'm nauseated at the thought of this new swelling of his larynx that has produced a voice so inappropriate for my small, small boy I see before me. I wonder if poking a hole through his throat would help that swelling deflate. Then maybe he would be back to speaking in that old, excited squeak.

And still, I answer his question with a hungry "yes," because I really want to. Yes, right now. Really bad.

He knows how to lay his arm out. It falls with a plop on the armrest of the sofa, and I compose myself by seeing how obedient he still is, even if he's feigning.

The needle is a tiny thing between my index and thumb, hot now from how tightly I've been holding it, careful not to drop it and lose it in the fabrics of my carpet. I've lost a few in the heat of it and later at night unpleasantly find them as I drag my bare feet to the sofa to watch TV. I do not want it in my feet. I want it in *him*, then in me.

He closes his eyes, and he no longer wonders if it will hurt like he used to. He's used to this and knows just how it pricks. The pain is just like the usual feeling of where his legs join his pubis, where his arms always rub against his armpits—the usual sensations of skin and friction that one grows so accustomed to they become phantom pains the body does not dignify with attention.

But I really, *really* want him to ask like he used to.

"Ask me if it's going to hurt," I say, my voice almost breaking.

"Is it going to hurt?" he replies monotonously, and I regret it instantly, even if he's being a good, obedient boy.

I don't know why his voice is so stiff, and instead of replying, I start going at it, start poking, the needle going in and out of his skin, leaving nothing behind, only a small hole I can't even see. I do it more vigorously than usual this time, and all I notice is a faint wince on his part, a little biting of the lower lip before he returns to being stoic, distant, the pain no longer joining us. The birth cord the pain once was between my hand, the needle, and himself is now worn and ruined, and I think that is why I choose to go even more relentless than before, perhaps the same way one desperately feels around a cold body for a heartbeat, or the way a lover pries the mind of his beloved with questions, looking for the answers he wants to hear.

Then I'm done, exhausted, and I sit back, ever so careful, more careful than ever, to not drop the needle still in my hand. That needle now has *him* all over it, and it is an essence that I must cherish for as long as I can. I even resist the urge to suck it, maybe even swallow it.

He rubs and scratches his arm, breaking more skin than I did, and I can tell he still has that old habit of picking at his scabs. Maybe he's trying to rub me off himself, but his expression belies nothing. I know more than anything he just wants to leave.

With a raised voice, I tell him to look at me, and those bored, wandering eyes fix on me as I take the needle and now work on myself, poking through my own arm now and making sure we retain the eye contact, ascertaining that he knows what I'm doing: That the fondling through his follicles, the pain that gave rise to his holes, every moment the needle met his skin and poked through, all of that now runs through *me*, my body greedily swallowing it all. I just repeat to him to keep watching over and over in low grunts, keep urging him to see, to feel, to *understand* that he's mine in that moment, that I am poking him into myself. Yet, I know all he can do is watch.

When we're done, I slip him $100 and tell him to leave, once more unfulfilled. I shut the door behind him, not knowing what to do with myself. I feel around my arm, trying to see if *I* really believe that I have devoured his pain and his injury and made something of his mine.

As I ask myself, all I feel is a limp arm, the skin wrinkling and scarring, and the loneliness of my own touch feels just like death.

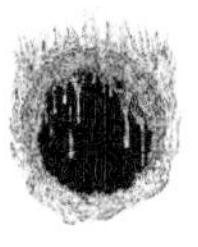

I need to make bigger holes.

I decide this that same night.

In the pool of cum drowning my belly button is where I see these thoughts. They're opaque, the color of dust. Every few hours something else sheds from my mind and flows out of me like another gristly fish, swimming straight into this belly button pool where it swims and dances in its ever-wet contortions, and I stare sometimes all night. Tonight, the thought swimming around is the holes. I *need* those bigger holes, because the ones I have been making are losing me my boy. The ones I've been making aren't big enough for him to really come out.

I get up and clean myself with a stiff dish towel by the TV stand. Then I walk to the living room. Half-asleep, I reach the couch my boy had just been sitting on hours before.

I bury my face into the seat of it, gripping the armrest so it holds me steady, for I feel I'm falling—falling through that dirty fabric, through the foam cushion and into the cool, limpid surface of a gray nothingness, and it's gray like my cum, gray like his dirty baseball jersey, gray like closing my eyes against a bright light.

I realize moments later when I get myself out of that static that I'm sobbing and holding my chest, and I'm feeling my hands and the pain between my knuckles saying they are eager to poke.

My boy won't even tell me his name. He won't tell me where he lives, what he does at school or elsewhere. I suspect that even his uniform is a lie. Countless times I've rounded every park, every baseball field, seeing many boys in uniform, but never *him*, and it gives me the urge to drag my hands through all those yellow-green lawns and search under every blade of grass to see if there's even at least a single drop of him. I don't know where he sleeps or what he does when he closes his doors. In my mind's eye I try to see, but my mind isn't strong enough to poke holes through those doors he shuts.

The *him* that I see when he marches into my home (and I tell him, *your home, your home too*, but he says nothing) is only what he lets me see, a faint projection, a stray gust of the true and unbridled storm that he must be in that inviolable sanctity he calls his privacy.

I want to poke holes through that privacy.

Big holes.

I want to see, and I want him to bleed out, and I want to catch every single bit through my own holes and pour him into me.

That is why I'm sobbing, holding my chest, decided that I need to poke a bigger hole so that all of him will spill out.

Then in the living room I watch TV in the dark, staring at fuzzy people moving like ghosts behind a film of white noise. I'm surrounded by the smell of my sweat. My clammy hands are shaking, knuckles still aching, aching to poke, sweating out all that angry, rotten urge. Then my eyes shut, my right arm resting where his rested, my buttocks pressed against where his were pressed, and I try to imagine this place he once occupied is now a hole he's left behind in the air of my house, and one which I'm trying to fill in, fitting into its contours, clenching my teeth and wishing I were smaller, frailer, wanting to wane away down to his size like hot swollen skin cooling down. I try and try, gripping the armrest, curling my toes, jaw clenched so tight I start feeling something burning behind my ears. Then I lick my lips, and maybe I imagine or maybe I don't, but there's a taste, a smell, a faint figure in the corner of my eye and I tell myself it's *him*, all over me, enveloping me, the darkness of his insides now part of my skin.

I do a good job of smiling and half-convincing, but in the back of my mind I know it's not true, and that's enough to leave me empty.

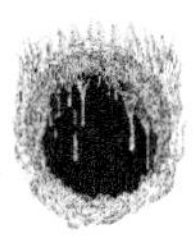

The morphine did its job. My boy is fast asleep, but I'm afraid he's no longer my boy. His head now hangs back against the backrest of the sofa. He's been like that for half an hour, and I've left him untouched. I don't want to touch him. I'm repulsed.

It's not my boy, but the aching persists, and I haven't let go of the needle. I still want to poke the holes in him.

It's a bigger needle this time, the kind for knitting, wooden but still sharp, and equally hot in my grip as the others. This one, I won't lose. I take a few steps toward him brandishing it, but then I decide that this is not the way to go. I need him to wake up first.

And so I wait to see if those eyes will look back at me and wonder what they'll look like shaking off that heavy and unnatural sleep, how his entire body will inflate again and resettle into the rigid, living form of his that I want to poke. Poking a hole through *this* now would only feel like stabbing with fury at water. I need his arm solid and awake, so it can give way to the holes I want to poke in him.

Now I'm genuflecting, carefully listening for some answer from him, much the way a hopeful and hungry beast might watch some pregnant prey, knowing there's even more meat awaiting to spring from that bulging womb—the birth of something large and hearty that will feed. I need it and can barely contain myself, hate myself for having drugged him in the first place, behaving like a cold idiot putting out his own fire, now desperately rubbing sticks to reignite it, hoping the wood hasn't frosted over. I start worrying that maybe heat has escaped this house forever, and then I notice, without thinking, I'm now pressing the needle against the softness of his arm.

I'm really going to do it.

Then he wakes up, head shaking, neck bulging like there's snakes inside, eyes trying to take in the size and heft of the strange room, trying to anchor themselves with familiar sights. I can see the recognition of his surroundings dawn on him by the way those eyes resettle into discomfort, perhaps an added fear at the realization of why he went to sleep after drinking my coffee, the mug still knocked over, the dark ooze of it like a bloodstain now long since soaked into the smallest tendrils of my carpet. His eyes are looking everywhere, up and down, and then maybe the uncomfortable pressure against his arm finally alerts him and makes those eyes fall on me.

And that's where I want them.

And that's when I start.

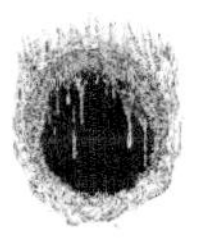

I know he screamed, but I couldn't hear anything. I know he bled, but his blood was just warm air running through my fingers. I know there's holes all over him, nickel-sized holes like eroded rock—wet, mouthlike, fattened holes of pink and purple stippled across the interrupted softness of his skin, all over his arm and down his back, just above the buttocks. They are ruinous, stygian holes that are selfish, jealous, even being so deep and dark they refuse to let me see inside. Earlier I brought a lamp closer to inspect, but the darkness in them is solid, immovable, like his insides are all coagulated shadows.

The needle broke, and I only noticed when my hand kept stabbing, but no more holes were being made, only my fist punching against what little knit-together flesh I left on him. I ran my fingers over every hole and found the other needle half lodged in a hole near his armpit, but my fingers are too fat to get it out. I think of pliers, but I have none. All that beautiful, wondrous, breathtaking essence of what was done here, all that pain and force imbued into that needle, dancing along its length to the rhythm of my poking—all of that is now just another thing he selfishly guards, his flesh now swelling around it, its grip tight, and it's like fighting clenched, wrinkled lips for a morsel of food they won't give up.

I see my boy is still alive, eyes peeled open, mouth drooling. Since I tore his shirt off to keep poking holes (in a single clawing, surprising myself with the strength with which I endeavored to remain uninterrupted), he is half-naked, only adding to his image of a shriveled, discarded knot of limbs, side bleeding and squelching with holes. I can't work on myself with the needle still in him, but I give it up as the swelling wound closes around it, sealing it behind skin desperate to heal. Now I just hold his face, and even with the last of his strength, he shifts his eyes away from me.

I feel terrible. I don't like what I have done. I want the needle, but I want *him*, too. There's too much blood, oily and black, more than I thought he would be holding inside. What big mysteries there are, I think then, hidden in the crock of the body, and one never knows how messy they are until one goes poking trying to spill them out.

I ask him to forgive me, but he does not respond. The only answer is his faint breathing and the slushing of blood and the echo of faraway organs humming through the holes like steam whistling out. Then I kiss him, but that feels wrong, so I stop. Somehow, his mouth feels like the one hole I should not touch.

Then I *really* feel his blood, and it's like drowning as I run my fingers over every hole, still feeling his light twitching every time I try to poke through one. Then I try to hold him all shut, but the blood is now unending, flakes of flesh catching under my fingernails as a scramble across his ruined skin, and I mourn that I did not hear a single one of his final breaths.

Then I sink like the previous night, and I think maybe the big coffee stain on the carpet is a vast sinkhole that has sucked me in without warning. I keep sinking, back into that gray pool of nothing, that static torture that drowns my head, except now I'm still holding onto my boy, a finger in each hole like the holes are lifebuoys cast out into this grayness to keep myself afloat. Now my mouth is pressed to another hole, and I think to blow into it, as if maybe I can control the wind that flows through him with my fingers at each hole and make a melody of him, play him like an instrument, have at least my own hot breath run through every smooth surface of his entrails, but only blood answers my lips—bitter, ugly blood enveloping my tongue. I almost vomit, but I keep my mouth pressed there and keep a tight grip on his holes, because I know they're what's saving me right now from drowning once more.

Then, I feel myself being dug out from my sinkhole and accepted into the give of his skin. He gives warmth to each of my fingers and to my lips. Now there is sensation where there had been none before whenever I'd feel myself start to sink. Deeper and deeper I'm digging my fingers into the soft mush, the feel of wet clay and turgid ligament as I'm uncoiling from despair, and though his outer body is cold and tightening with death there is a warmth I can still feel somewhere inside. Farther, now my nose pressed into a hole, too, my tongue stretched and reaching as far in as it can reach, nudging through briny muscle and watery fat, I start to feel that there really *must* be something in there, something sacred and unseen that my eyes can devirginate and my wet, trembling hands can possess. I don't know if I will find it, but I'm digging—digging through all of him.

EMPTY NESTERS

First, he liked the way the smell of ground coffee crept in from the kitchen into his waking nostrils, bringing in warmth and familiarity. Next, he liked the smell of clean linen, always insistent, and Mary always leaving his shirt and pants ready by the bedside. For 30 years her hands and feet had moved with dexterity across the rooms and hallways of that home, even before dawn, to ensure that everything was in order, and, though he hated to admit it, she worked to *his* liking. He had never even had to ask her to do things, would not have *dared*. Yet she simply decided it should be so, and she once offered as explanation, "That's love, I guess." That did it for him. *God, I love her*, he thought to himself for the millionth time, finalizing his morning stretches. Through his shame at her hard work, and through his own guilt that maybe he did not deserve such a woman, he affirmed and affirmed, *God, I love her.*

Making faces in the mirror, sticking his tongue out and winking, more out of unfading boyishness than anything, he eyed his profile and persistent gut salted with white hairs, thinking, *You're getting old but not too old, Charles*, and chuckling. He threw another quip in as he sucked in his gut only for it to bounce back out. *Going on*

55 but don't look a day over 52. He urinated, shaved, and rinsed out toothpaste residue and mouthwash. He put an end to his lonesome thoughts, dressed for the day, and searched for Mary around the house. Not in the kitchen, not in the living room, his content smile dropped in realization of where she must really be spending her morning.

He found her, as expected, in Jack's room, hunched over and kneeling next to the bed going through the contents of a small cardboard box, the one token their son had left before moving out. Standing at the doorway, Charles could barely make out her faint sobbing as she gently heaved up and down. He knew she was quieting her cries for his sake. He stood there a bit until he could no longer take seeing her like this and knocked gently on the open door to announce his presence.

She foolishly rushed to close the box up, knowing he had already seen her in disarray. Then, she chose only to wipe her wet eyes and stifle her cries further.

"Morning, honey," she muttered in a broken voice.

Wordless, Charles walked over to her side and knelt down next to her. They embraced, and she curled a shaking arm around his neck and cried openly. It had always been the same, a ritual of her own that went along with every stage of their Jack growing up. It had happened when Jack left to college. It had happened when he left for med school. It had happened yet again when he purchased his own home, and now, with Charles remembering the gift-wrapped toasting flutes they had bought two nights ago for the wedding, he realized he should have known it was coming one more time. He did not cry over Jack's successes the way Mary did, but of course he knew it was not his success that Mary truly bemoaned. This was about the family splitting up, farther and farther with each milestone. Even though they frequented each other, even though the love was still there, the distance accentuated the pain of not being together. Perhaps *because* there was love overflowing, it hurt more. The love was all over the home, on the wall marked by Jack's growing height, in the boy's empty bedroom, in his baseball cards and baby clothes. Charles felt himself choking up but held it together. It was not that he did not feel like crying over Jack, too, in his own wistful way. It was that he hated thinking of these things, so he quite simply didn't.

"Honey, it's okay," Charles thought to say, and her subsiding moans told him it was only his gentle words she sought that morning, and he was more than willing to give. "We're gonna see him in three weeks and hug and kiss and have a few drinks. We're gonna be laughing our heads off in Hawaii, dancing by the ocean." At this promise, he felt a little chuckle fall out from her pained throat onto his shoulder which she pressed her mouth against. He felt her breath like the comfort of a lukewarm day creeping in with the morning sun, and he laughed a bit, too.

They spent that morning going through the box, the mementos, Jack's tassels, medals, and the many pictures, their boy growing older and older before their eyes with every flip of the photo album, but those rosy cheeks, those wide blue eyes were always the same, always full of joy and forever robbing their hearts of adoration. Now Mary saw the same contents of that box with laughs and relaxed eyes, laughing a head-falling-backwards laugh at his inventive Halloween costumes, with an "ooh" and an "aww" at his baby photos, his school dances, his first employment headshot—cleanshaven, sharp, a confident and powerful smile beaming back at them. For hours, they passed his old belongings around like communion, leaned on each other, and when it was time to put the box away, it was as if nothing had happened. It had cost a late breakfast, but Charles and Mary kissed tenderly, and he smiled and kept smiling knowing they could always make it alright for each other.

Going downstairs to start their day, they paced through their sprawling cabinets filled with awards and souvenirs, all from Jack, who loved to excel in school, and had loved college wrestling even more. Charles couldn't help but remember that first day they had laid eyes on their future home, how her one and only protest had been, "It's too big for our little family." Now, reclining on the living room sofa, he felt like saying, "Told ya so," chuckling to himself, which she didn't hear. He had known back then that only a house this big would be able to fit all the greatness and success and joy their son would bring. *Jacky boy, you make me proud*, he kept thinking over coffee and eggs.

In the living room that lazy afternoon Mary sat curled up reading a book she had picked at random from the shelf. Charles thought it was *Walden* or *Pride and Prejudice* from the corner of his eye, but he was much too intrigued by the developments in some home renovation show, playing at a respectful volume on the living room TV, to really check. In their peace and contentment, and admittedly old age (*Aye, that one always stings*, Charles thought), the hours slipped by every day. Soon enough, though it seemed they had just gone through their morning rituals, dinner was already in the oven. Mary had figured she could work a few neurons with her book while it cooked, and Charles had agreed he could lose some with his show and his six-pack (although years had passed since he could stomach more than two beers at a time). However, even ingrained in his show, every commercial break was a breather for him to lean back and really take it all in.

He felt quite self-reflective that day. Perhaps it had been the episode in Jack's room, how he had nearly cried, and how it had decidedly made his head bow in gratitude. Sure, he'd given it his own hard work, had invested his life in his job to ensure his family was cared for, but he couldn't help but try to itch some spiritual aching that had been building in his mind. They had never been religious. They had agreed to let Jack choose on his own—no crosses or bibles unless they were gifts from their more conservative neighbors, and even then, they were shyly tucked in the lower, less-visible shelves. *But I'll be damned,* Charles thought, *if there isn't someone out there watching out for us.* Then, by reflex, he eyed the sign next to the fireplace that read "Blessed" in curling, ornate letters. Mary had been doubtful about hanging it up, but Charles had concluded that he simply liked the message, and it didn't have to be religious. "It can simply be the truth," he had told her the night their neighbor Rose had gifted it to them. *Blessed,* he thought. *Well, that's exactly right.*

Shortly before the oven dinged (though it was less a ding and more a marimba jingle that came with a brand-new oven touch screen and brand-new headaches for the oldies—*they had the oven right, no need to make it more complicated*), Charles had fallen into an admittedly buzzed rumination as his eyes fell on the mantlepiece by the fireplace. It was crowned by a curvy, senseless sculpture, of turquoise and jade, that he had bought for Mary many years back at TJ Maxx. He recalled how he had felt like such a success, to be able to buy that for her even though it had no use, when she only wanted it because it was pretty, and because she thought it would fit the décor. *When you buy your wife the useless thingamajig, well, you're doing okay, I guess.* He wondered if that was prideful, ugly, wasteful. Sometimes he did feel an ache having such a big house, buying the thingamajig, making those exuberant trips and purchases. But in their love and affection, things like that mattered little. Staying grateful, he thought, was his goal for the approaching, concluding years, the onset of his final days which he hoped would be at least plentiful enough to be happy, with enough time to play around with future grandchildren, things like that. he couldn't quite picture yet what his grandkids' faces would be like, but he knew there would be the same love and ambition in their eyes as in Jack's. He reclined on his seat once more and waited for dinner to be announced. And he thanked *someone*, whoever it was.

The oven roast hit the kitchen counter when the phone rang. Charles picked it up. It was Joseph. He said to Mary, "It's Joseph," and she decided she had to tend to the garden outside anyway before the sun went down. In his age, Charles still had to do some business now and then. Mary found her way to the garden briskly, and Charles agreed to some of Joseph's words over the speaker, then hung up.

He opened the cellar door and descended through the dark smell of shit. He felt their shivers all about as he shed the smallest light from his phone on their naked, wet bodies. Some were against walls like pillars, some pressed down to the floor like concrete. When one dared cry and scream he let her have it with the stick, and then no others dared. He covered his mouth and nose with a handkerchief and went about sifting halfheartedly. Joseph had said, "The brownest, biggest tits you have," and it echoed in his mind as he searched. He found one that fit the description and dragged her by the hair to the row nearest to the stairs for better lighting. He made her stand straight though she barely could, top heavy and bruised, but not too bad. He squeezed her tits, checked her cunt. She did not scream but made her presence known by the rattle of chains on her shivering body. She *knew* not to scream. This was the one he had broken in a couple months back, the belly already swelling like ripening, dirty fruit. Joseph would slit her cunt open and have her shit babies slither out soon enough, and that fetched good money as well. Finishing with her cunt, he let the body fall against the dirt floor and poured a bucket of cold water on her. She whimpered so he kicked her, and then she wheezed something in some language that was like silence to him, but he kicked her again anyway. He knew she was really waking up with the cold water now, so he let things run their course.

He almost ran back up the stairs but kept it together. He walked back with confidence, authority, for he knew they were looking. The iron door shut with a dirty clang behind him, and he popped some Nature's Bounty in his drying lips as the locks were resettled and Joseph was dialed again.

An hour or two passed and Joseph left the house in a cloud of dirt. Mary had been resting at the garden bench, knees soiled and neck tense. Dinner would have to be reheated that day, but that was usual. They never knew when Joseph would call. Charles joined her with a tray of cheese and wine and a gentle back massage and the good news that the thing with Joseph was done for the day. They said nothing for a while and then spoke of the flowers, the beautiful blooming begonias and how it looked just like in her dream. She had always spoken of that dream, of a garden, a home, them sitting in old age still madly in love. As he softly kissed her, the waterworks almost came again. *God, I love her*, he thought again, his hand on her cheek, still smelling of soap despite her hard yardwork. A fulfilled dream, once blurry, ethereal, but now solidified, physical, running in real-time before their eyes—that was what their life was. Still, it felt like a dream: airy, delightful, and so tender. They nibbled some cheese and threw the rest to some nearby nesting ducks. The wine was enjoyed, and they marched back inside holding hands.

Though a bit overcooked due to reheating, Charles proclaimed, "Dinner was perfect." She smacked his shoulder with the softest touch, a smile and a chuckle that said, *You devil.* The phone rang again, and Charles answered as usual, smiling at the recognition of that enthusiastic, "Hiya, pops!"

He spoke to Jack for a while as Mary eagerly hovered nearby, waiting her turn. Charles spoke of how the plans for the honeymoon were done, and how Jack should not worry about a thing except the sacred mantra: *Happy wife, happy life*. Jack only half-snickered at the recognition of dad's favorite phrase, not amused by its novelty (as he had surely heard it a lot), but by the fact that he finally understood those were words he would soon uphold with pride.

Charles, normally content with mundane talk, knowing his son was alright, was still in that contemplative state that had carried over since morning, so he thought of making his earlier thoughts known, even if it was out of character for him. "Jacky boy, you make me proud," he said candidly, his voice softer than usual.

Jack only answered, "Dad..." his voice trailing off, breaking. The two said nothing and Mary was already tearing up, having overheard.

He handed the phone off to Mary, who spoke of every detail of her and Charles' lives, or as much as she could cram in before Jack had to go back to work. She said a thousand "I love you's" that she meant with all her heart, and Jack knew how she meant them, but still, he also knew that what his dad had said over the phone had been the biggest testament to their unfaltering love that the old man had ever dared state, and so, through his phone "goodbyes," he felt his father's words carry him to a comfort where he could easily remain until he saw them again, as if the very words tucked him in goodnight like in all those past nights of his childhood.

Huddled up on the sofa, half-watching a movie, Charles and Mary kissed. Sometimes they still had relations, but it was just as joyous to simply share company, just as intimate, just as fulfilling. Charles grabbed her breast, but it was a gentle caress, careful and slow, guided more than anything just by the need to hold her, and she knew this. They locked eyes and giggled like small children for whatever reason. They went back to the film and never touched the hot cocoa Mary had already made. It was getting late.

Back in bed, another day had gone by, just like that. They changed into their pajamas, never shying from seeing each other naked. *She can see this bag of bones and hanging meat,* Charles thought, pulling up his pajama pants. *And she still loves me. God, I love her.* With every wrinkle known, every hair and every fold explored, not much seemed to matter except the calmness of the fact that their bodies were close. Crawling into bed, soft and warm against a particularly chilly night, Mary thought to read some more of the book she had started earlier, and Charles thought only to look up at the ceiling, head pillowed in his hands, and then to just close his eyes, relishing the peace.

The book was shut, the lights were out, and the two curled over each other, tired and content, the creaking of their bodies joining like two puzzle pieces completing a whole. Mary thought it weird that Charles was so ingrained in feeling her hand, playing with her nails, running through the creases. Still, she knew it was not worry making him fidget. She could tell he was just interested in, just devoted to, her hand.

And it was his hand to have. She swore on this.

In the dark, against the whistle of the outside wind, Charles said, "We've done alright."

Mary said nothing, but he knew, even in the dark, that she agreed with a sleepy smile.

USER

Ma's jockstrap fell down to her knees. The fucking thing was too big for her skinny hips, and she didn't want to eat that night, either so she wasn't gonna fit them anytime soon. That's how I knew it was ma, old and wrinkled ass cheeks that didn't look right, making me soft and frustrated. It was no longer my Baby Sid like I'd seen for a split second, but ma laid supine on the mattress, short black wig pulled too far back with grey, dry hairs showing, arms this way and that, doing a low panting that gave me pause. Her pussy flaked with drying lube like was like smelling salts, really waking me up. I reached over the bed and turned down The Germs.

I pulled out, cock sore and red because maybe I'd gone too hard that time because I'd found this one angle where it really was my Baby Sid taking it in his tight little ass, not ma. Then I turned her around. I met her eyes and tits too big to be Sid's (nothing was right, not a goddamned thing, something always out of place). I saw something numb in those eyes, maybe a little angry, that told me it was over.

I went and got a damp towel and patted her forehead, which was hot, but not with fever, so that was good at least. Then I grabbed some of the cheap toilet paper I'd bought the day before and cleaned her a bit. The paper was coarse and looked like it hurt, but she needed cleaning. She smacked her lips, and her breathing went down to about the sound of a whisper, and I thought she said, "Thank you," her legs and between them no longer hurting, I bet. I dressed her, and I then let her be.

I went to chat with Fred on my phone in the living room. I sent a message first.

"Hey hottie xD JK!"

I was being all playful but was still feeling some hardness and hotness at my crotch, feeling sexy and like toying at something with Fred, but he didn't answer just then. I turned the TV on and signed into Netflix, but I found nothing good. There was never anything good, and I felt sick of paying for nothing good.

I turned to the phone again. Fred had replied.

"Hey."

I didn't feel like typing, not being good with words and spelling sometimes, so I sent a voice message, in a low voice that I wanted to be sexy and hot like hot breath in his ear, real breath that he could feel.

"Hey, just thinking of you. Hope you're okay, bestie. Did you get the movies I sent you?"

He took a while like always to respond and that made me frustrated, but at least ma was asleep. If she had been awake making all her weird noises, I would've lost it. Fred typed his answer back, not giving me his warm, sexy voice in reply like I wanted, and that made me frustrated, too.

"Yeh I got them."

Again, I was no good at typing just then. "You're not just using me to get free movies, are you, bestie?!" Then I laughed a little at the end of the message, but I really wanted to know the answer.

"No of course not."

His response was quick. I smiled, then went to my computer, blasting The Germs again with some Agent Orange. I went on Amazon to see what else I could get him. I found some DVDs about karate, and I remembered he said he'd done some karate years ago, so I got him those. $56 total, but Fred was good, so he deserved them. Fred was always good, and I knew I was just fooling around with him with all the sexy stuff. I knew he was married. I knew he had kids. I didn't mean anything, just being silly, but while rubbing my shaking hand on my cock I knew maybe I'd want to see him soon. I knew maybe I'd want to see what could come up with him.

"Still no cheap flights to Denver :(LOL"

I typed this time, not bringing myself to say it, knowing I'd sound sad.

He stopped answering. Probably busy with his kids, so I fell asleep watching a true crime show I'd seen a million times. I said in my head a million times I'd cancel Netflix and stop paying for nothing good.

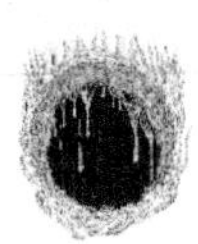

There was a leak the next day, pouring really hard from the apartment above and dripping down our bathroom light. I told ma, but she wasn't in any mind to know what to do. She hardly ever was during those days, and it frustrated me. I wanted her to come back, so I grabbed her by the shoulders hard and shook her and said, "Ma, our fucking ceiling is leaking! Ma, look at all the fucking water!" but she looked at me like I wasn't there. Angry, I hit her, and I wasn't happy about that, so I said sorry. I pretended it didn't happen.

She said, "It's alright."

I did smile at that.

I called maintenance. I was so, so frustrated, the words barely coming out right, wanting them to fix their stupid shitty ceiling we were paying a fortune for. That's what I said. They said someone would be right over.

I had to hide things around ma's room. I had to hide the dildos, the pictures on the wall of Baby Sid Vicious doing his sexy little poses in his white briefs, his bulge telling me to peel the pictures, scratch them so I could see his cock while he played the bass strings with those skinny, rigid fingers. I had to hide all of it because the bathroom was in ma's room, which I always hated, because sometimes she locked herself in there and getting the key and dragging her out was a hassle. She was being dumb those times. I even hid the wig, since whoever was coming over could still ask questions about it, and I wanted no questions. I had to hide leather stuff that I sometimes used for the times with Sid, things that really hurt and made noise, even above Darby Crash's painful growls. I was furious when all was put away. It would take forever to put back.

The maintenance guy came—an old, Asian fat fuck that barely spoke English. In his weird face it was hard to make out what he thought or if he had suspicions already, and that made me frustrated. He looked at me weird, too, when I answered the door in my tattered Adolescents shirt, nipple piercing showing. I was happy for that, because I knew he avoided looking at it like one avoids looking at the sun, the word "faggot" probably dancing at his tongue if he even fucking knew the word. He also stared at my tattoos, of things like sigils and death and all manner of things from my time learning witchcraft, from my time conquering enemies with unspoken arts, things this sorry Asian cunt could never understand. I knew I could kill this fuck if he tried anything. I knew I could sew his throat shut with just a wish—not that anyone would know what his broken ass English was trying to say if he tried ratting me out anyway.

That's how I kept the things in those walls a secret—by being careful, and where I wasn't careful, occult gods guarded my cherished things. This was a pact I had made long ago.

But the fat fuck didn't say anything, barely looked around, just breezed past ma's room and into the bathroom and watched the water now landing in a big Halloween cauldron I had lying around.

"From the apartment above," he pointed up while saying his fucked English answer. *No shit, Sherlock*, I almost said, but I just said I already knew that. He said something else about the leak, about the guy who lived above leaving the water running, always causing trouble, and something about being careful because wet wires inside the ceiling never dry, big risk of fire maybe, but just then my eyes were on ma, who was seated in the corner of her room, and I saw her mouth wide open, and I knew she was starting her noises again, soft first, then louder and louder like crying and yelling. You'd think it was Sid getting fucked right there with all the whimpering.

Fat fuck turned to her, his narrow eyes growing with confusion.

"She has dementia," I said quickly, not knowing if he was wondering, but I wanted to explain it at once.

He looked embarrassed, which I liked. I was glad he at least knew that word. He scrambled for his fucked words and said sorry and that he'd be back tomorrow. Then he left, and I gave ma a good shake till her eyes got sleepy.

I knew there was a dark god, a dark star watching over me, massive and cold with arms all about, deciding things, guarding things, knowing fat fuck wouldn't tell anyone. Ma stopped her noises, and I groaned as I took out all the things again, rearranged everything back to how it was, back to the pictures of my Baby Sid I could stare at all night, feeling hard already as I taped them up, feeling that sexy, warm good feeling of the crotch of my jeans growing tighter. I looked at Sid, already rubbing my bulge, and I noticed ma looked away like ashamed, but I knew she wasn't, or maybe a bit. Maybe in her head there was still a little shame she could feel, and I left her room and let her be because that made me a little ashamed, too. I was frustrated by that.

In the living room, I thought to call Fred. I tried video calling three times, but no answer. Minutes passed and I was going to try again, but he messaged me just then.

"Can't talk right now man. Sorry. Goodnight."

I smoked maybe five cigarettes in the living room, the smell now being just the normal smell of the place, the walls around the window yellow from all the smoke I was trying to blow outside, sometimes missing. Just then, maybe the smoke tried to remind me of something important, but I forgot everything. The smoke made everything grey, dizzy, and I fell asleep.

I half woke up because I damn nearly set the house on fire, the stick still lit between my fingers. Again though, I knew, many dark and cold hands were running all about that place, guarding them. I'd been sure to summon them there with a spell they'd feed on for years and years. Those hands would never let their guard down.

"Santa brujería," I muttered to myself, almost falling back asleep and now dipping into the little vodka that was still lying around. "Santa Muerte, fuerzas negras." Things like that I had to tell myself now and then to make sure the guarding hands stayed put all about me. It had taken me so long to learn how to say it all right in Spanish.

I fell back asleep and woke back up at around 9. I went into ma's room, gave her the pills, got Sid all ready and laid out supine, Baby Sid, lubed up with my two fingers, warmer and warmer in there as I rubbed around his hole and pulled on the jockstrap elastic (tightened with a rubber band this time), making his little tight ass bend upwards and submit to me, all for me, my baby, presented like a feast. I got the wig on him and got naked myself, twisting my nipples and the piercings stabbed through them. I grabbed Sid's hand to twist them for me, but it was so wrinkled, so frail, so cold. It didn't feel right so I threw it aside. I tried looking at his face, but it wasn't right, either. The nose wasn't right at all. The nose bothered me most, for some reason. It looked nothing like Sid's nose. *Is this or isn't it Sid?* I hated having to ask myself that when I was already twisting and stuffing his fingers in my warm, hungry hole. I was getting frustrated, but my hardness never went down, so I said, *Fuck it.*

I got an ass cheek firmly between my teeth, looking up at the wall and those pictures of Baby Sid with his bulge playing the bass, and I got so hard I thought I could fuck him all night as Darby Crash wailed on:

We must bleed.
We must bleed.

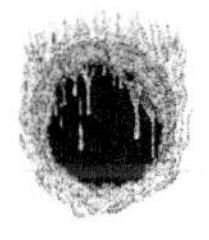

"I don't use anymore," I said over the phone, because Uncle Ronald was asking about ma again. I'd just gotten her social security check in the mail, got the app where I could just take a picture and the money was there in my account. I wondered how they did that, and then on top of that my payment for being her caretaker came in. I wanted Uncle Ronald to shut the fuck up so I could talk to Fred and see what else I could send him. Fat fuck came back in to fix the leak, and I had already hidden and rearranged things all morning, so I had little patience for all this. "I've been clean for years. I told you a million times."

"I care about my sister, Bruce," he said in his rushed voice, like there was any hurry at all. I also fucking hated being called that, Bruce. He didn't know I'd been christened "Hot Toe" by the brujos and brujas of the streets in Oakland, those who knew what real and ancient power was, figures that could kill just by touching. I'd seen it myself, and I knew I could harness that if I really tried, and I could make Uncle Ronald cough blood at once if it was my wish. I fucking hated "Bruce." But I held back, not wanting to make his head spin just then.

"She's fine, but you know she doesn't talk much." He didn't budge so I put her on speaker.

Ma said nothing, only groaned and then she started drooling, which frustrated me. Of course I'd have to clean that up.

"You see?" I said triumphantly.

Uncle Ronald said goodbye.

I sat ma up on the toilet and left her peeing while I tried video calling Fred. No answer, but he started typing.

"Sorry, with family, what's up?"

Not good at typing just then, so I sent him voice messages. "I just wanted to check that you got your new gift, bestie!" My voice was low, sexy. I hoped he liked hearing it. I hoped it would go into his ear and stayed there, warm and tightly coiled in there like a slug in the mess of his brains where it wouldn't rub out. "I had some more money come in, so I want to see what else my bestie needs."

Fred took a long time as always. I was rubbing my cock the whole time, looking through his pictures where he barely showed his face, but glimpses of his beard, of a veiny hand, a sturdy finger, made me rub rougher and kept me hard, not wanting to think about anything except his low, low voice coming through like a soft kiss I hadn't felt in a long time.

He replied in voice message, and I pressed play so fast. "Hey, man, I got the DVDs you sent me." He sounded doubtful, which was frustrating. It was not the strong, gruff, sexy voice I knew he had. "It was very kind of you, but honestly, I'm starting to feel bad getting all this stuff from you. I'd feel better if we just chilled, got along respectfully as friends. You said you take care of your mom, so why don't you use the money to take care of her instead? That would make me happier. Sorry, I don't want to sound ungrateful. I appreciate the kind gestures, but let's slow down on the gifts, okay?"

I typed back, throat tightened shut, fingers barely managing.

"Its ok"

I hurled the phone across the room.

I threw ma on the bed like never before, ready to force the pills down her throat. I couldn't wait for her and her schedule. She struggled, and I was angry. I was angrier than ever, it felt, looking up at Sid's pictures, but that didn't even help, only got me harder and made me meaner, teeth already biting at ma's lips in case she tried making any more noise, switching panicked breaths back and forth between our mouths, both of us not knowing what was going to happen. I didn't feel the tickle and good hurting around my crotch, but it was weird like it was pure, unbridled anger pouring out of there through the hole at the tip like pissing, burning through the length of my cock, burning through its hardness as I dislocated her jaw popping the pills in there, my own stronger fingers like cocks forcing her open. I felt the snap, heard the crack around her jowl like cracking some hard fruit open, and the pills went down.

I got Sid ready, tight ass squeezed tighter in that jockstrap. Mike Palm was singing through the loud, loud speaker next to the bed:

It's getting harder every day
To think of better things to say
About what's going on around you
And what's happening inside you.

I felt the words vibrate up and down me and really felt a weird, gross kind of high school heartbreak feeling as I thought of Fred while I readied the body under me. I hated when those feelings gut stuck in my guts like that, felt like some bad food my body couldn't shit out. Sid's hands that looked wrong were tied at the front with leather rope. Then I got naked. I was hard but didn't feel it. I just felt angry, burning, burning hot and alive with the sigils down my arms, the skulls and the eyeballs and the bats and the runes speaking to me, because they were angry, too, feeding me bad energy, ancient hatred that made me harden like rock, curling my hands to fists, grabbing Baby Sid by the waist, eyes shut tight as I fucked and felt the bones around his hips fall out of place like a China plate breaking.

For the first time, I talked to Sid. "Do you like it? Do you like it?" It fell out hot with my panting and groaning like fire dancing along his crooked back.

Without answer, I fucked until the bones jutted out like fingers pressing outward from under the skin of the hips, and every time I tried to push them down, the hole tightened around my hard cock.

Then Mike Palm finally bemoaned as my cum shot out like a deadly bullet up those chafed guts:

Everything turns grey.

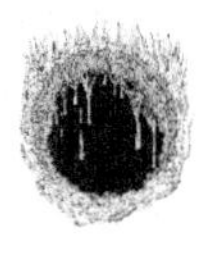

First thing the next morning, I googled:
"Best revenge dark spells"
"Most mortal brujería"
"Best cheap lube"
"How to hurt someone long distance"

"What's not allowed USPS"
"Rhinoplasty for senior citizen risks"
"Made at home casts"
"Sid Vicious"
"Sid Vicious shirtless"
"Sid Vicious naked"
"Sid Vicious deep fake porn"
"Sid Vicious smiling"
"Sid Vicious"

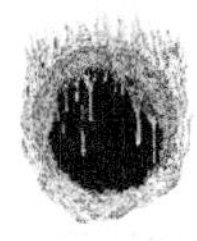

They asked a lot of questions at the social security office. Ma was there, but she was of clearer mind than before. She still couldn't talk from the swell around her jaw, which by the divine force of these watchful hands of mine they never noticed. They only asked her yes and no questions and she nodded or shook her head, sound of mind. She even smiled with a wince, and the lady at the desk smiled back. I held her hand the entire time. I knew they liked her a lot.

Driving us back, I got us both ice cream from Dairy Queen. Mom gurgled something, but I couldn't understand her. I got her a chocolate sundae, and she liked that. With her shaking hands she tried to scoop it into her mouth but eventually I just fed it to her, still holding her hand, holding tighter than I thought I was, with tears in my eyes that I wiped away before she saw. She ate the whole thing, even asked for fries, so I got her some.

Back at the apartment, the damp smell from the leak was finally starting to go away, and the smell of my cigarettes was coming back full force. I let her sit on the living room couch, still chewing on the sogging fries while I put groceries away. She said "movie" twice. I said I understood but I was busy then, getting a little frustrated, but not too much. I think with ma there was always a little prickling, a little fuzzy coat of angry and frustrated, but it was light enough to be ignored, so back in the living room I kept scratching my arm from that prickling and told her "okay."

We put on *Dirty Dancing*, her favorite from when I was a kid. She was watching in silence, the brightest her eyes had been in months. I almost fell asleep with my head on her lap, watching the bodies swinging on the TV, and then with one of those wrinkled hands, she started playing with my hair and going "shh, shh." I could tell it hurt her mouth, but she kept making the sound.

I let ma play with my hair, feeling good and like I was a kid again, a young, young kid and like it was *her* turn to put me to sleep. Then I saw her eyes start to close like she was falling asleep, too. I lowered the volume on the TV, then ran my hand around her leg where my head was pillowed. It was soft, frail, the cast around her hips hugging her tightly, looking silly like a big, rock-hard diaper, which made me chuckle, but I could tell it didn't hurt her anymore. With all the pills I gave her I could tell it didn't hurt at all. I lifted her dress a bit and felt her bare leg, and it was a good kind of warm.

Then I laid her supine and now we were both lying on the couch, and I kept touching. I kept running my hand up and down looking for something, the last of my tears finally shed. My fingers gripped some spots tight, pinching, and thinking how soft, how weird, how good, *good*, then weird again. Other times I pinched harder spots, things under the skin that felt like muscles, tighter, harder, and that made me think how hot, how *sexy*, my eyes clutched tight, afraid to see but loving the touch of something human of hardened muscle beside me, lying with me. Then I felt my fingers go into ma, not Sid but ma (and that phrase echoed really loud in my head, *not Sid but ma*, and felt ugly), and it was as wet and hot as Baby Sid, and when I finally looked up with open eyes, like staring directly at the sun, I saw ma's face, slack-jawed, staring back with eyes as dark as nothing. I think maybe I said to myself, "This is good. This is good."

I got up and let ma be. I went to her room, to our bathroom, the place we shared most—between pissing and shitting we met more than any other time—and looked for the shaving razor I had used on Sid's legs days before.

There's a picture of Sid from a Pistols concert in Dallas, Texas, from the year 1978. When Sid came on stage, the audience saw, horrified, that he had carved the words, "Gimme a fix," across his chest with a razor. That was the same night he called that Dallas audience "cowboy faggots." I always thought Sid looked so sexy that night, all cut up, but the cuts were hot like deep, scabbing tattoos on his smooth, smooth skin, half his face bright red from his own blood, too.

I remembered then, walking back to the living room with ma, that maybe that was the picture (or one from that same concert) that first made me hard when I was a kid. I remembered Sam, the older, blond punk guy next door when we lived in Oakland, that sexy guy with the skin-tight pants and popsicle-red mohawk, the bulging crotch of the jeans always a darker, more aggressive color. He was the one that first told me about the brujería his friend Pedro's mom did, something about killing chickens and burning sage as he made a spooky "ooooo" sound with his soft, soft mouth. I think it was in one of his magazines where I first saw it, maybe that same day that he invited me to smoke weed in his bedroom, and later on when he said he felt light from the smoke he let me play with his crotch until he said it got too weird. Maybe while I was playing with his crotch I looked over my shoulder and saw that image, that red, red blood, Baby Sid looking dead eyed like I was just then, looking flushed with blood and sick of being there, standing, alive for just a few more months, and all this while I was feeling Sam's denim twitch and writhe inside my tiny fingers, like a scared newborn puppy looking for the warmth of my hand.

So anyway, that's what I did to ma that night. That's how I tried to cut her up, at least, not the same—always close, but some things were wrong, like always, so I got frustrated. The writing was all crooked, and I rolled my eyes. At least you could tell it said, "Gimme a fix." I also think maybe just the red, red blood was too much and too bright, blinding me and keeping me from seeing ma, drowning her, fading her away into the background. I was also drowning in that hot, red ink, bathing my own black tattoos of sigils and dangerous, monstrous, unnamable things while I fucked and fucked, and he bled and bled.

When I felt myself slip into that swollen, broken ass, tossing the cast aside after tearing it from him, I saw the skulls along my wrist and the bloodshot eyes down my forearm grow darker than possible, dark as deep black cracks dividing my skin, and with words that rang only inside my ear, they gave me all the power, all the glory, all dominion over the living, and very close ties with death. That sounded right, so right, and I knew that night I had risen to a new way of being as my prize danced along my cock with newfound wetness.

I went blind for some seconds. Not just shut eyes, but blind, everything grey even when my eyes peeled open. When I came, shot that furious load as it dissolved with blood and shit, the sight came back, and all was untouched, Baby Sid crying softly from the good, good fucking. I just slipped my pants back on, didn't even clean off the blood. I don't know why. A lot of things stopped needing a reason.

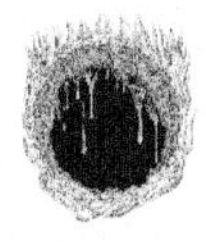

I tried Fred again, and he replied.

"Hey what's up?"

"You been quiet"

"Sorry. Lots of things going on in my life right now but didn't mean to worry you."

"Its ok"

"Did you get angry at me? You can be honest."

"Of course not bestie <3"

"Okay that's good to hear! Finally at least some good news in my life, haha."

"Were close friends right"

"I'd say so! As far as the internet goes I guess. But yeah, man, I trust you."

And that's when I sent him the picture of me, the picture of me with my nipples rings twinkling like stars, like I was as big and mighty as the sky, and of Baby Sid laid supine and bleeding an angry red beneath me, silently begging for a fix with the wrinkled, pale slits across his torn belly.

"What u think ;)"

No response.

No response.

Blocked.

Messages greyed out.

Everything turning grey again.

Then more red. Much more red. I didn't even see ma at all that night, just red. Just Baby Sid there bleeding, getting fucked, and I knew the blindness was crawling back into my eyes, the blindness really settling in my sockets which were fuming with steam from all the dark vigor my guarding hands burned across my tensed-up, bending back.

The tip of Sid's nose fell on the carpet like a small pebble. Then my sight gave out. The razor click-clacked against the counter after I dropped, and it was the only thing I heard before my ears went numb from the screaming, louder and more broken than any human scream, feeling Sid's arms shaking like a baby out of air from throwing a tantrum.

I put on *Sid & Nancy* and fucked for hours and hours. Through all the fucking, I smelled something like smoke, but not from cigarettes. Baby Sid stopped tightening, stopped gripping my cock, like a final breath slipping out.

Gimme a fix. I kept thinking to myself as I kept going, really meaning it, really wanting to dig something out of there with my hard cock, the fix I needed to use again, almost going fully blind even after shooting cum across the wetness of that newly flattened snout.

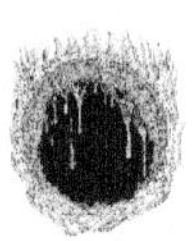

"Hey you fucking piece of shit here I am emailing you this like were fucking coworkers or some shit because you blocked me everywhere else. No biggie LOL I dont care about a fucking loser like you except I do care for fucking losers that also owe me money because they turned out to be nothing but FUCKING LOSER USERS

LIKE YOU! All those gifts I ever bought you and all the things I helped you out with. even sent you stuff when you said your kid was going back to school and I never heard thank you from that little fucker either but thats besides the point. Don't worry though lmao I keep all my bank statements and I'm going to bill you for every last cent that you owe me you fucking piece of shit. You know what you were doing, telling me you were bi, telling me how youd jerk off to your male classmates, how you never got too experiment as much as you wanted, how you were curious all that shit because you knew you were gonna fool me and get me to buy you all that fucking stuff without ever planning to even meet me or be with me. WELL I GUESS I GOT TIRED OF PAYING FOR NOTHING GOOD. NOW YOU OWE ME AND IF YOU DONT PAY ME YOU HAVE NO IDEA WHAT I CAN DO!!! You laughed and all that when I told you I'm a brujo but this time ur gonna see ur gonna meet the devil himself. You keep laughing and not paying me back and ull see. u will see. I know ur scared"

When I sent that email, barely able to see what I was typing, I heard the same loud tearing sound I know Sid also heard when Nancy died. It was the same pain, the same pain that was also buried in those ever-wet scars begging for a fix as I buried my nails in Baby Sid's chest and felt the hot blood run down my arms, licking my tattoos, giving them strength, giving them that dark, powerful magic. That entire night, I stopped seeing and only felt my fingers still digging through the hardening skin that I knew was Baby Sid still tight in my grip.

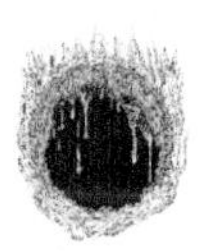

Mastectomy.

I had been trying to remember that word for hours.

I googled it while preparing a Priority Mail box headed for Colorado. I laughed to myself. Then my phone alarm went off.

Ma's appointment (Dr. Marasco): 1 PM-2:30 PM

Deleted.

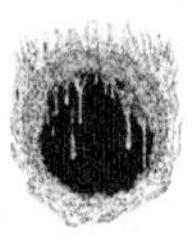

Sewing was easy without seeing. It was like sewing onto fabric, but the skin was tougher, messier, wetter. My fingers got tired from looping the needle around and around and even forcing it in was work. I don't know how straight it looked, but the wig was held firmly in place. Now it was like the real hair growing from a real scalp, even wet with blood just the same. *Real skin.*

That night is when I stopped remembering much, except that fucking Sid had gotten tougher, tighter, then good again once my muscles really went down on him and made his give in, got him nice and smooth again, licking that cold earlobe like a metal piercing dancing on my tongue.

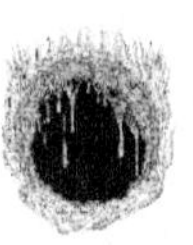

I wanted to go to V-Mart that morning when I remembered Fred said the sushi there was good, but I couldn't drive. I could see nothing, but I wanted to be with Fred, even if just like that—even if just by going in and grabbing the sushi and imagining it would look just like that when *he* grabbed it with *his* hands. I really wanted to look at his hands again. I was forgetting them in that angry, lonesome grey of my sockets.

Fred, Fred, I said to myself on repeat like I was shaking the body of a dead friend, too tired even to fuck my Baby Sid.

I sent another email, maybe the same night. I didn't have to see. I knew this one from muscle memory:

“*Fuck you fuck you fuck you fuck you fuck you fuck
you fuck you fuck you fuck you fuck you fuck you fuck you
fuck you fuck you fuck you fuck you fuck you fuck you fuck
you fuck you fuck you fuck you fuck you fuck you fuck you
fuck you fuck you fuck you fuck you fuck you fuck you fuck
you fuck you fuck you fuck you fuck you fuck you fuck you
fuck you fuck you fuck you fuck you fuck you fuck you fuck
you fuck you fuck you fuck you fuck you fuck you fuck you
fuck you fuck you fuck you fuck you fuck you fuck you fuck
you fuck you fuck you fuck you fuck you fuck you fuck you
fuck you fuck you fuck you fuck you fuck you fuck you fuck
you fuck you fuck you fuck you fuck you fuck you fuck you
fuck you fuck you fuck you fuck you fuck you fuck you fuck
you fuck you fuck you fuck you fuck you fuck you fuck you
fuck you fuck you fuck you fuck you fuck you fuck you fuck
you fuck you fuck you fuck you fuck you fuck you fuck you
fuck you fuck you fuck you fuck you fuck you fuck you fuck
you fuck you fuck you fuck you fuck you fuck you fuck you
fuck you fuck you fuck you fuck you fuck you fuck you fuck
you fuck you fuck you fuck you fuck you fuck you fuck you
fuck you fuck you fuck you fuck you fuck you fuck you fuck
you fuck you fuck you fuck you fuck you fuck you fuck you
fuck you fuck you fuck you fuck you fuck you fuck you fuck
you fuck you fuck you fuck you fuck you fuck you fuck you
fuck you fuck you fuck you fuck you fuck you fuck you fuck
you fuck you fuck you fuck you fuck you fuck you fuck you
fuck you fuck you fuck you fuck you fuck you fuck you fuck
you fuck you fuck you fuck you fuck you fuck you fuck you
fuck you fuck you fuck you fuck you fuck you fuck you fuck*

you fuck you fuck you fuck you fuck you fuck you fuck you
fuck you fuck you fuck you fuck you fuck you fuck you fuck
you fuck you fuck you fuck you fuck you fuck you fuck you
fuck you fuck you fuck you fuck you fuck you fuck you fuck
you fuck you fuck you fuck you fuck you fuck you fuck you
fuck you fuck you fuck you fuck you fuck you fuck you fuck
you fuck you fuck you fuck you fuck you fuck you fuck you
fuck you fuck you fuck you fuck you fuck you fuck you fuck
you fuck you fuck you fuck you fuck you fuck you fuck you
fuck you fuck you fuck you fuck you fuck you fuck you fuck
you fuck you fuck you fuck you fuck you fuck you fuck you
fuck you fuck you fuck you fuck you fuck you fuck you fuck
you fuck you fuck you fuck you fuck you fuck you fuck you
fuck you fuck you fuck you fuck you fuck you fuck you fuck
you fuck you fuck you fuck you fuck you fuck you fuck you
fuck you fuck you fuck you fuck you fuck you fuck you fuck
you fuck you fuck you fuck you fuck you fuck you fuck you
fuck you fuck you fuck you fuck you fuck you fuck you fuck
you fuck you fuck you fuck you fuck you fuck you fuck you
fuck you fuck you fuck you fuck you fuck you fuck you fuck
you fuck you fuck you fuck you fuck you fuck you fuck you
fuck you fuck you fuck you fuck you fuck you fuck you fuck
you fuck you fuck you fuck you fuck you fuck you fuck you.”

The USPS returned my box. The mailman even waited around to see me personally and explain what could have gone wrong, but he only saw me, I know, blinded by the fury of dark and bitter gods, stained, disheveled, and I heard him say nothing else.

Back inside, the house was a mess, the floor still greasy. Three blind attempts with the mop and the grease wouldn't leave. I threw some trash aside and placed the box on the table. Cutting the packing tape with the razor made me think of earlier, of the same crisscross cut across the breasts, opening like flowers and all the fatty blood spilling out, the floor now slippery forever it seemed, all the grease left on it like a new skin.

In the box I felt the severed fingers hard and wrinkled like old carrots. I threw it out.

I fucked that night, too, I think.

I can't remember.

But I feel like I would remember the smell, the cold, the dark.

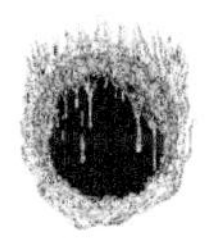

The smell of smoke was there again while I fucked another day. The twisted trunk of Baby Sid like a tree with all its branches broken was bouncing up and down against my cock. It was heavy like that, bulky and hard to grab like that. That was the only thing I could feel. My arms felt fattened, gorged with the brutal strength I knew now possessed me.

I was dancing, my hips circling, really giving this tight little twink bitch my all, this little rocker faggot, this little virgin fuck that was my Baby Sid, not even needing pictures anymore because Baby Sid was now enough, was now a clear, clear image, even when I couldn't see—a clear image built through braille as my cock never left his hole.

Maybe it was now even starting to look like Sam, too, who knows, with the same skinny, skinny frame, the same boyish size and tight hole. But always face down. I couldn't bring myself to feel the two big black blotches like giant cigarette burns across the chest, "Gimme a fix" now illegible, even with touch, like graffiti painted over by bigger, rougher gashes.

The phone rang, but it wasn't Fred. Fred hadn't called in a long time. I don't know who it was.

I just said I was busy.

Hot Toe, I remembered my baptism, in cat's blood, in a back alley in Oakland with the powerful brujos and brujas making their fingers dance along me and all inside me, chanting as they laughed and jeered:

Hot Toe.

Hot Toe.

Hot Toe.

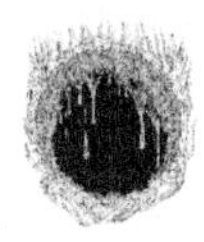

Fire. I knew there was fire then, real fire. At first I thought maybe the heat was because the caking blood stains around my crotch were finally becoming red-hot fire. But it wasn't that. Of course not.

I tried to think of what had been different that day. Maybe it was when I told my phone to play the new voice message I got and it was Fred, threatening, saying he could have me jailed. I didn't care.

I kept thrusting. I was a blind beast, a blind monster, using and using that heavenly little hole as I pleased with the energy bestowed on me, not needing sight, not needing reason, just needing this tight, stubborn hole trying to push me back out. Then I felt the heat, real heat from a real fire gusting into the room like hot breath out of Baby Sid's mouth.

I looked down and was reminded, finally, of something with clarity, like my eyes really opened after being glued shut for days, and the orange brightness hurt me.

I remembered the red, drooling snot from ma's cut up nose, making tiny sounds like a squirt gun or a clogged spritz bottle, till it went quiet forever, and that really brought me back.

Now that silence was really there, right at my waist, tingling up and down my cock, waking me up, seeing that I was fucking something that looked like a skinned deer, in some spots deep grey and spongy like bad cheese.

Then I *really* saw the flames coming from that light fixture in the bathroom and licking into the room—"*Wires never dry*" thumped in my head in a broken, fucked up Asian accent.

Something inside convinced me, recoiling from the red pulp about my thighs, that the gates of Hell were opening for me like I had always heard them say at those masses ma loved, at those church events that promised damnation for sinners, fornicators, sodomites, and when I'd hear that word "sodomite" I'd clutch ma's hand so tight because it sounded like a big and scary word. Then back in my room I started trying to grip that same soft, warm hand that was ma's hand for comfort again, but all I felt were mangled, dry bones with the tips cut off, jutting from her palm as the mattress started turning a burnt black.

I hugged ma. She burned inside my arms so fast and so bright that my eyes shut again. A smell of garbage enveloped us, choking me with how thick the smoke made the stench. My eyes and nose burned like that, and then my mouth and tongue felt a vivid, hot pain forced down that didn't even let me say, *Baby Sid, Baby Sid.* I thought those words like maybe he'd still be there waiting in the dark of my eyelids.

But no. There was nothing, and then—

Everything turns grey.

PART 2: CUTS

IN A HOT CAR

Inside the car there was only the sound of a little knife hard at work.

Outside, the strong winds were as loud as whippings, diving in from the east as if yearning to land and be buried under the clouds of hot sand that danced around the desert ground. The sun was finally setting, but it was leaving the skin of the earth searing, swollen with heat that barely managed to cool down for a few hours deep into the night before daylight resumed its punishment. A skittering from the night fauna signaled that it would soon be dark enough for them to resume their dominion, their chases and conflicts that adorned the sounds of nighttime. However, the last sunrays still managed to ignite the plains in a painful orange glow that warned and said, "Not yet. Not yet."

The parked car stood out like a tooth in blood, the white of its metal reflecting light back at curious buzzards who, thrown off for a second, knew to keep their distance, but remained eternally curious, decidedly greedy, circling the darkening sky due to the strange smell of carrion rising from a window that was cracked open only a fraction of an inch, still allowing for an unbearable heat to cook inside.

The stench had also attracted other waking noses and claws, curious to see, come nighttime, what strange gift or trap had been set so clearly in the midst of their hunting grounds. These wrinkling snouts, these ears standing rigid and fully alert, were already weary of the road, that hardened gash of stone, like a black scab along the smooth beige pelt of the ground, on which fast and loud things often ran, faster than any natural thing that had ever raced down those plains, making the surrounding dust, once undisturbed for many heavy years, rise and fall day and night with winds of their own. Those lightning-fast things had claimed countless of them in single, body-crushing swoops. Other times, out of grace or carelessness, they left behind husks and wrappings that smelled and tasted vaguely of blood or grease, and overall were good and filling things to eat. Now, the dwellers of those plains stood intently watching this thing which appeared to be one of those very fast and deadly beasts, except it showed no signs of its awesome speed and made no cues that it could pounce or stand its ground at all.

They would wait and see.

Inside the burgeoning, ever-sticky warmth and heavy stench of meat going bad, Luis had managed to carve out a hole as big as his eye through the rear seat. He had worked quietly, making sure the knife made little noise as it scraped through the rough upholstery. The last thing he had been told was that silence was needed, and so silence he gave, even if all the previous screaming in the trunk made it pointless. He had been holding onto the last instructions the short, tattooed man had shouted over the confused and pained moaning, his impatient voice rising, using a heavy boot to make sure they took up the least amount of space possible in that trunk. Like an angry mother scolding her children, he had shouted over and over, "Callados! Todos callados!"

Luis had been holding on to that, like the urge to be a good, obedient boy drowned out everything else. It made him feel safer following the orders of grown adults after such a long time of doing everything alone. He had felt comforted knowing his life was finally in someone else's hands when he found this car that would cross him to el otro lado. So, he had stayed quiet. He had stayed quiet even when he had felt the car stop. He had stayed quiet even when it stood still for such a long time, the heat in the trunk starting to boil and mix with the stench of the others, with nervous, beer-ladened belches and the humidity setting in their pits and cooking inside the men's shirt collars. Then, when he had heard the frantic footsteps getting farther and farther, leaving them behind, dissolving into the growing worry and pained wails brewing around him, through all the agony of his fellow passengers, he had not made a single sound.

The other four bodies crammed around him had broken that sacred rule, had screamed and clawed soon after they came to a stop, yelling, "Ya nos llevó la chingada," finding no way out, and then Luis felt the lady lying next to him strain her breaking voice as high as she could, like elastic about to rip as wetness dripped around in the dark, and everyone knew there was blood from her ripped fingernails from trying to claw out through the metal trunk door that would not budge. Luis had felt some of the warm, thick drops fall around his mouth, and he had stuck his tongue out, embarrassed to be tasting this lady's blood, nauseous from the now unbearable heat and stench, but grateful for the metallic moisture on his tongue. Then, the sweat began and made his clothes unbearable, gritty and tighter, slimy with lip-ripping salt, and the four other, larger bodies had begun to sweat as well, and writhe, and all was wet and filthy, arms and legs and gaping mouths vomiting out more cries, all feeling like the world was about to rip apart and spill out their bodies, contorted and seeped in filth, turned to mud. In his nostrils, Luis could have sworn he had smelled the exact moment each of the four around him breathed their last, musty breaths.

Now the reinstalled quiet was an abandoned dream, clinging to Luis for nothing else other than being obedient, and sticking to a plan which had clearly failed. It somehow made the stench worse, with no more movement to reassure there was still maybe a bit of hope or life stuck in there. The silence only told him that there were now four dead, decomposing bodies around him, and that air would soon run out.

In the constant thump inside Luis's head that said, *cállate, cállate,* he had begun to pray, to ask Diosito for an answer to his predicament just as everyone around him had, the two older men there with him even in their last sighs having desperately called for the glory of God, for release, for expiation, for the fresh air they all know was only inches away, yet unreachable. Luis wasn't sure if he believed in *Him,* wasn't sure if his attentive praying every night had just been because his mother had always told him to do so. Already age 12, Luis had gone many nights without praying, those nights like wormy holes eating away at his faith. But just then, when he was lying still in that oven filled with quickly stewing bodies, he had found himself praying and praying like trying to mend those holes with desperate, untrained fingers. *Por favor, Diosito, por favor, ayúdame, por favor no dejes que me muera, por favor, por favor, no me quiero morir todavía.* He had learned no other way to talk to God besides begging, and so he had begged, drawing in thin breaths of the putrescent, thinning air of men and women boiled alive all around. He had begged and begged.

That was when, like the divine answer so few of his people had ever received, he had remembered the knife in his pocket, the same one he had stolen from the tin under his mother's bed filled with dad's old stuff the night before he ran away. Though dizzy and disoriented, eyes useless in that hefty darkness, and quickly running out of energy, he had reached into his pocket and had felt the still cool blade between his fingers. Then he had realized he could cut, dig his way through, and find at least some fresh air to fill his tortured lungs. He had had no time or mind to feel guilty about not having told the others of this tool, but he hoped they would understand—understand something he himself could not detect or define, an urge to break out of there that was not heroic, but his own selfish, primitive need to live, like a muscle spasming. Still, before he had set himself to the task, he had searched with his hands for the eyes of the lady atop him to close them shut out of respect, but all his trembling, blind hands had been able to find were limbs thrown about him, and a shapeless wetness all about, not just from blood, but other liquids the bodies had begun discharging once they settled still. He had had no time to feel horror or disgust at this, either. He then had stumbled and writhed and moved as much as he could, positioned himself against the backseat, the great wall that squeezed them shut into their unseen deaths, and had begun cutting.

And now he had this hole. He still could not break through, for a hot metal spring box still stood in his way like cell bars. Still, he pressed his mouth against the metal coils, like suckling a nipple, ignoring the burning at his cheeks and lips, and breathed in countless painful gasps of air filtered through the dirty foam cushion, coming in irritating and dusty, but still invigorating his life which had almost slipped away. In filling his lungs with more semi-clean breaths of fresh air from the tantalizingly close freedom of the outside, he felt his voice revive. First it came back in small gasps that accompanied every breath, in and out. Then, he felt something way in the pit of his stomach dislodge. With still painful gasping, his voice itself boiled, bubbling up the feelings crammed way in there, feelings of fear and anger and loneliness and death. Erupting, pushing through his breaking throat, they emerged in loud, shrill cries.

This went on and on.

The sun outside was still setting.

The crying alerted the hunting wildlife further, to the point where they halved the distance between their kind and the weird creature by the road. The skies were still a noticeable mauve, the lone red veins of the sunrays beginning to thin to nothing. Soon, so soon, their friendly darkness would descend, rousing them, readying to tear at their target shred by shred, slowly at first, then in their united effort to know its insides. The annoyed buzzards still circled in delusion, knowing they would be roosting soon, and would only get whatever the morning left from the feasting of those on foot.

The land dwellers felt, along with the darkness descending, a newfound wakefulness that roused them further. Even if their eyes were not as developed as the snouts and ears that guided them through the darkness of their hunt, they still perceived the enveloping shadows that brought them close together, familiarizing themselves once more with the sightless night that would soon mean working with each other, always knowing where the others' feet were stomping, where the others' sets of jaws would strike and cover their target piece by piece. It was now almost in unison that they gnashed their teeth, perked their ears, and scratched their claws on the sand, claws hungry for blood and meat.

Luis's crying had died down, but he still heard nothing outside. Although the skies were darkening at a quick pace, he saw the opaque light filtering through the seat's cushion as intense compared to the insides of that car trunk. Yet, more than anything, he saw it as *close*. The air had helped tremendously, but even then, still buried in darkness and the waste of the other bodies, it had only helped him think more clearly about his predicament, how he still had not come up with a way to really escape, and how close he still was to joining the waste that laid all twisted behind him. He had removed all of his clothes, sitting there naked, ashamed, taking breaks from sucking in the fresher air to press some of his naked parts against the hole, alleviating the warmth around his pits, his stomach, and his feet with the maddeningly light breeze that felt even icy against his sweat-drenched skin.

The praying in his head had ceased. Like a spoiled child given his candy or his toy, he now clung to his life without gratitude or subservience, but only an anguished need to keep said life in his grip for as long as possible. Being alive now felt prickly, unfitting, like a yoke around the neck dragging him along in his frustrating need for more air, more space, his body growing too large and meddlesome for that dark, tight hole that had now been marked as a grave. He only dared think of those bodies there with him in small glimpses. He remembered the older men only as the friendly smiles cast his way and the tired, lulling heads sitting about him in the bus ride to the meeting place with the tattooed driver. He had gathered them up outside a gas station in Mexicali, and there he remembered the old lady only in the fragmented image of her trembling hands, twisted with arthritis, shaking her head while handing him a smashed taco she had kept at the bottom of her backpack. "Ay, mijo, qué barbaridad," she had kept saying as she fed him, almost like scolding him for his actions. Luis had eaten this part of her lunch greedily, barely daring to look up and meet her eyes to thank her, knowing it would only break him down. Now, those were discarded things, smiles that would never resettle on those gaping mouths, not another thought of random kindness guiding their hands or feet. He was alone, and that loneliness settled with a cruel and morbid finality as he kept watching the light beyond the seat cushion really running out.

His mother had told him not to go. She had known there was trouble when the older guys started asking around town to see who wanted to cross to el otro lado, a promise as easy as saying it, like there was only a distance to cut through and not a Byzantine net of legalities and prosecutions, and there had certainly been no mention of the immovable spot marked by death he now gasped in, either. How lightly those older men had moved around, checking pockets, running numbers household by household, having recruited maybe two or three other kids from Luis's town, kids he had known for years and who had slipped out of their homes at night like him, following these men, never to be seen again. When they had come to his house, his mother had protested, almost running them out with a broom as they laughed and departed. He had hated his mother then, chained to her shuffling around that old house falling apart, chained to bemoaning everything as the roaches and scorpions overtook corners of the bedrooms and kitchen. He knew now he had escaped mostly because this image of his mother was the most painful thing he had ever felt in his young life.

What had been most alluring to Luis about those men was their *grace*. He had admired the way they seemed to almost float through the town, like they never had to even touch its dirt, only gliding by like gods on their procession, casting their urgent invitations on Earth. That same night, Luis had stolen all the money he found in his mother's room along with his dad's knife, leaving the yelling and beatings he would never hear behind. With no time for food or extra clothing, he had set out in search of those men.

He had found them drinking near the outskirts of the town. Luis snuck inside the tavern, and the tattooed one with the gold along his arms and neck had recognized him, sorry to say that the other kids from Luis's town had already departed on an earlier bus, but surely, yes, surely, there was still time, and the money that Luis was carrying had thankfully been just enough.

Luis punched the hole in the seat in anger, feeling the heated metal spring box tear through his soft skin. He could not see the bleeding, but felt its wetness, mixing with the grit of newly forming blisters. How tantalizing it had been, after his first adult drink which they bought him ("yo a los 12 hasta perico me metía," one of them had proudly stated between laughs), after that night of hearing these men exchange stories of their fortune, their journeys, the easiness with which they crossed that border that to them was just about moving forward, plowing through decrees and authorities through their own clandestine pathways. They were powerful men, Luis had recognized. They were nearly magical, and there they had been, in the flesh, treating Luis as one of their own.

"Esta movida no es pa' cualquiera," one of them had even said. "Pero tú traes finta de que sí aguantas, plebe." He had included Luis into their lifestyle, expressly said Luis was now moving above the ground like them, stomping through the air across the vastness of the place beyond the miniature world that had been his whole life, stomping above fences, walls, towards the promise of their riches.

And now, here he was, naked, soiled by waste, by dried tears and snot, lungs burning with the miasma of those who had chased the same glory, those who represented the same ensnaring defeat that was soon approaching.

Luis hit his head with his weakened fists. He told himself over and over: *But I'm* not *the same as them! I'm young. That's what one of them, the fat one with the mustache, had said: Todavía estás morro, tienes chance todavía... And I have my knife.* He reached for his discarded pants, pulling the knife out and holding it close to his bare chest.

As he cut through the foam cushion, he felt the daylight slipping through his fingers, urging him to work faster, the blackness beyond ever threatening. As he felt a chunk of the cushion give and the first hole he had made widen, he tossed the knife aside and instead began clawing at the opening with his bare hands, no longer concentrating on steadying his breath. Instead, he began screaming in fury, his light arms surprisingly warping the spring box, bending its stubborn skeleton until the space between the coils was big enough to let his arm squeeze through. In some brief but feverish, heavy seconds, he struggled with the foam as if on his last burst of energy, his body ready to double over and melt away into that wet death at his knees. In that struggle, the foam cushion tore away completely in uneven shreds, and then the fresh air was all at once there, pure, and the dimming light of the sunset's end was brighter, blinding. Without hesitation, not allowing himself to be lulled by the intenseness of this newly revealed daylight, Luis knew there would be a way to fold the backseat forward. They had not owned a car in years, but when he was very young, his dad had shown him how to do it, pulling a small switch to make space in the back to fit the large tools he used at work. Now, scrambling to make his arm reach the space between the headrests where the switch had been in his dad's car, he searched blindly for that key to his freedom, like fruit dangling from string beyond his famished mouth. Finally, his fingers found the hard plastic mechanism, and in one frail, clumsy pull, the seat bent forward, landing in a dusty plop as the rest of the car revealed itself, all bathed in dim blue light. It was as still as if hell and death had not just suppurated in its rear end.

Like with a wounded vagitus, Luis spilled forward, naked, drenched, wild-eyed and screaming out of sheer anger and triumph. With this also came the newfound feeling of shame as he saw himself naked for the first time in the dying dayglow. Crawling on all fours, he did not dare look back at what he knew would be a hell scape obscenely illuminated by this newfound excess of light. He did not wish to know any of those four's deaths in detail, thoroughly haunted already by what he had imagined through touch. He only made sure to grab his knife and underwear from behind him as he lunged forward into the driver's seat. Covering his privates and placing his knife on the dashboard, he reached for the ignition, but no keys were lodged in. He had never driven, but with eyes peeled back by fear, he was willing to maneuver pedals and steer straight down the road in frenzied speed if it meant getting somewhere, getting anywhere.

Still searching for the key, he had found a metal tumbler in the cupholder. Tearing off its cap, he drank the lukewarm coffee (warmed only by the heat all about) greedily, and it was like nettles running down his throat, sickly sweet and thick, so that the third large gulp came back out, mixed with drool and splattering across the passenger seat. Semi-satisfied, Luis then cranked the window handles, rolling all four down and allowing the hot breath of the desert in, feeling cool in comparison to the oven inside. Deciding to resume his search soon for anything (and he really meant *anything*), he allowed himself the luxury of sitting still and basking in the new spaciness and hefty wafts of air that he had had been denied for hours.

Finally bringing his eyes to focus on the world beyond the windows, this was when Luis first noticed the coyotes. He was at first only looking at the vastness of faraway mountains, blurred by the heavy dirt traveling in the wind, astounded by the proximity of the outside, his for the taking if he were to only plant his feet out of that car. As if hypnotized by this prospect, eager to downright bury his face in the hotness of that new sand, his fingers had traveled to the door handle, ready to pull and make a run for it, for the land he had paid to be taken to, the promise of prosperity that had been so cruelly tossed his way with no plans of fulfilling it. Anxious to burst out, he fell into complete stillness when he heard the first snarl. He barely dared peek his head over the driver's side door, looking clearly through the open window at the slobbering jaws of a creature, skinnier but longer than a street dog, something about it accentuating its wildness, its bloodthirstiness, its pelt a dark gray and dirty brown that seemed as if also made of dirt like all else.

Luis began rolling the window up slowly. He only let out his held breath when the handle rolled no more. The coyotes had not made a single movement. He felt a bit of relief coming from this small triumph, yet he was aware of the three other wide-open windows all around him. As quietly as he could, he slipped over to the passenger seat, the entire time half-expecting a frothing muzzle to fly in and snap at his neck in a single, deadly second. Once this second handle was within reach, Luis noticed just how many of the animals surrounded him. There were four at his left, three at his right, and as he rolled the passenger window up, trying his best impression of sereneness as he looked straight ahead, he noticed three more staring back at him in a watchful stance atop a boulder. He still did not dare turn back, even if just to see if any more were there. The passenger window rolled all the way up, but Luis noted how some of these hungry creatures were already scratching at the ground, waiting for some indecipherable signal to goad them into jumping into the car with him.

Slowly, he crept backwards, still facing forward, fully aware of the other danger in looking back. With numb legs still unused to so much movement after being crammed in the trunk, with cramps settling along his muscles through the strained labor of such awkward movements, he finally felt the hardness of the folded backseat beneath his buttocks as he settled on the left side first. With the same calm, calculated flicks of his wrist, the third window went up inch by nervous inch, and when it hit the top of the doorframe, Luis noticed, feeling lightheaded, that he had not been breathing the entire time. He also noticed the stench and heat, which had diminished once he had broken out of the trunk, returning and overpowering again as he resealed window after window, as if now even the entire car were not enough space, and the nightmarish clutches of the dark trunk were now extending all about him, Luis having only managed to expand his grave rather than flee from it.

With the slowest scooting, Luis now leaned against the right-side rear door, and growing sloppy with his technique, taunted and whipped onward by the finality of sealing out all outside threats, he worked in a brusque manner, pulling and tugging at the window handle as his breathing grew heavier.

The angry, humid snout of one of the coyotes flew in through the two-inch crack of the window still left open. Luis hurled his hands away from the window handle as if it burned him, crying out in terror as the animal's drool sprayed downwards at his cheeks in thick drops. The jaws snapped viciously, searching for the stinking meat that made its nostrils flare with hunger. Chomping at the air, growling and screeching, the coyote tried digging deeper inside, its eyes still on the other side of the glass but now for the first time noting the scared child weeping inside. It finally retreated, realizing, humiliated, that it would not get anything done this way.

Luis did not notice when the coyote scattered away to rejoin its brethren. In the final moments of daylight, as he had backed away from the hungry animal, his head had recoiled forcefully and by accident settled his gaze right on the carnage behind him, warped by the failing light, but rigid enough in its still visible details.

He did not see the four bodies. He only saw a giant, brown mound blistering with limbs and faces, twisted like masks carved on wood, bloated bodies covered with wet, gray hairs, skin blotching with purples and greens along the bottom as their rotting blood settled down. The mound seemed alive only by the glistening sweat, blood, and other discharges of light yellow and faint pink that made it almost glow under the tranquil, serene moonlight parting the night skies.

Luis screamed, raw eyes refusing to close, until his sanity unwound thread by thread, with the last rigid lynch pin tearing especially hard, taking consciousness along with it.

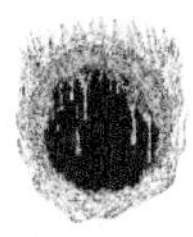

The night held only hungry things crawling closer and closer to the car. All other affairs had been paused—the birds roosted, owls hid in the cover of low twigs and branches, and lizards and hares all burrowed in the safety of their homes, having made it unscathed another scorching day. Only the loud screeching of the hairy beasts crawling on four legs resounded as the moon and low winds beckoned them to unite and spread their shrill song across the desert. After the effort of one of their kind, they had noted that it simply would not do to charge head on. Although darkness finally awoke their hunting instincts, revealed the secret pathways perceived only through the mist of moon and starlight, they had no hope but to wait for the thing inside to give them another overt opening. Frustrated, they howled and screeched in defiance, dispirited over being at the mercy of the panicking, weak thing inside, yet persistent, somehow knowing that it might be *really* worth waiting for.

Inside the car, Luis had felt other bold coyotes approach sporadically, headbutting the sides of the vehicle, hearing their sniffing filtered just across the car door. Even after the first attacker had managed to push its maw inside, Luis had still left the window cracked open just a bit, letting in outside air that made his imprisonment barely manageable, the stench now stuck deep in the fiber of the seats and persistently crawling closer to the front driver's seat where he sat. When he had managed to tear his gaze away from the bodies, he had crawled in a trance-like state to the front, curling in his seat and sobbing himself to half-sleep.

He yearned for his mother's beatings. He yearned for her anger to rain down on him, overpowering him, protecting him. Alone, naked, he did not feel like who he was when he had been in the presence of someone like his mom, someone from those last days, at least three or four days ago feeling like entire lifetimes away. He felt like something trashed instead, something with no amount of dignity to ever face someone like his mom again. He had been reduced down to a whimpering baby, a child to be carried home and spanked. His final hope now was that the tattooed man had not gotten far, and perhaps authorities on whatever side they were on would trace his path back to him.

And then what? He asked himself. *If I'm en el otro lado, get thrown back far from home and then get lost, no choice but try and cross again? Or, if I'm still far from home pero de este lado, get placed somewhere when they can't find my parents? In one of those dark buildings where abuelo Chucho said they touch kids and beat them and kill them because they have no parents?*

He knew waiting would only mean further humiliation, further hardship, or perhaps something even worse than the jaws of those hungry coyotes. He slapped himself with this thought now and then, as if trying to rouse another course of action. However, he was paralyzed, sobbing even when no more tears would come out. After a few more moments, he felt the warm liquid discharged around his legs. Would the smell of fresh piss somehow alert the coyotes that something inside was still breathing, preserving itself fresh for them? There was yet more cause to raise alarm, beckoning him to act quicker, but only more sobs followed.

Maricón, he was also telling himself. He *hated* crying. He hated its itching, burning feeling on his face, and he hated the shame he would cause anyone if they saw him like this. He thought again of those men that had come to his town, about their tattooed arms and gold adornments, and how strong they had seemed, how certain of their step, of their place above the rules, above playing things straight. He found himself incredibly embarrassed, the source of the redness on his face shifting from fear to shame. He was a maricón, a useless half-man, sin huevos, castrated and yelling like a girl for the coyotes outside to go away, for some migra gringo to come and save him and give him his due reprimand.

"Eres hombre. Ten huevos," was the last thing his mom had told him, begging him to be man enough to not leave her behind. He also felt shame from having broken her last wish, for giving his mom a daughter, a useless, ballless mariquita sin calzones with no money, no success, having tossed their savings off a cliff before he himself jumped. The howls and screams of the coyotes outside continued as the whippings from the wind grew heavier as well, and in that instance, Luis plunged his knife straight into the palm of his hand, holding his weak maricón screams back with his tightly gritted teeth. To him, those howls and screams sounded like jeering, like the dumb, starved animals outside knew just what was eating him: His lack of manhood which stomped him down into the seat of that putrid car. As he drew the blade back out of his flesh, he drank from the pooling blood at his palm and relished his own taste.

As the humiliating howls persisted, Luis thought less and less of his mother and more about the burning pain in his hand, and from that worming sensation of burnt and open skin came the hollow, raging anger that began to erupt inside him again. He cursed everything he knew, holding his knife close to his chest, over his bare chest covered in the flaking stains of the coffee he had retched back out. He cursed God, and he cursed the dead passengers there with him, and cursed the driver that had abandoned them there. He cursed his dad for dying and leaving them poor. He cursed his town and its mired, always hungry people. He cursed the migras out there probably looking for him, but most likely not. He cursed the border, the journey there, and out of everything he cursed, the only thing he left intact was his own mother, instead just carefully setting the thought of her aside as he got up on his knees.

When his bare feet touched the sand outside, Luis was surprised by how calm everything was. All howling ceased at once when he opened the car door, and the shining eyes of the coyotes reflecting moonlight all stood rigidly fixed on the small, half-naked body stumbling out into the cooling ground.

Luis tried his best to stand with pride, his dry, red eyes (a sickly black under starlight) staring fixedly at a void beyond all the hungry coyotes, into something distant, maybe not real, that was all the same comforting to him. The knife trembled in his hand, and his grip would not tighten. His ripped lips muttered half-composed words, words that had started as incantations of courage and manly strength, but were now tattered against the open, naked outside, against all those hungry jaws awaiting him. Still, he tried to stand with pride, because even with no marker, no sure way of knowing whether he had really made it to el otro lado or not, he had decided that he indeed had, that this was new soil for him to conquer, for him to claim what had been promised to him, what he had paid for, what was rightfully his. His toes curled in, as if the sand they raked inward were the first claim he made of his dominion over this land.

The first excited coyote that leapt at him missed the tip of his knife by a few inches, its yellow fangs nailing successfully into the softness of his neck. Encouraged, the others followed, and as the clumsy, wounded body flung its arms blindly about, others took the chance to leap into the open door, sniffing around the rest of the bodies, finding nothing appetizing left of them, some particularly bold ones nibbling at some parts before deciding it was all inedible. Instead, marching back outside, they joined the ones left to the task of overpowering this lively one.

One by one, the synchronized bites and claws came as the small body tried to stand its own limited ground. Not when two clung to its neck did it topple over. When a swift claw knocked the sharp object from its tired hands, the blade not having managed to land a single one of its drunken swings, the body fought on with bare fists, bouncing uselessly against toughened pelts and brawny legs. The body did not double over, not once, and all the while it fought until all jaws, in their united effort, finished tearing it asunder, flying off to their eating corners after a short spurt of red mist was swallowed by the wind.

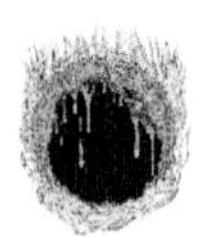

Officer Aguilar had a report to write after they caught the bald punk covered in tattoos in his filthy pissed pants, running across Highway 98 towards Mount Signal. Aguilar did not have much to add regarding this individual: Just another alien smuggler with a rap sheet full of all things that could be violated along the border.

With his interrogation, although advised by counsel to answer "yes" or "no," the entire story unraveled, as it often did, and agents were sent to look for the abandoned car. Found not too far from the arrest, the most noteworthy things that rang back to Aguilar were the stench and the level of decomposition. Even the hardest-stomached agent lost his lunch that afternoon as the open trunk belched out the mess of pulpy bodies boiled by the heat.

According to testimony during the interrogation, and due to evidence of children's clothing left in the trunk, there had been four adults and a minor involved. However, no evidence ever turned up as to the whereabouts of this child, and with verbal descriptions from Mr. Tattoos, they were still pending the hiring of a sketch artist. Aguilar scoffed at this thought, knowing that news of a lost child would get all the wrong mouths talking and asking questions, demanding things beyond the control of their overloaded department. In the light search the agents had performed the day the vehicle was identified, only a knife turned up as further evidence in the nearby surroundings. A child lost in the desert was surely dead, and he saw no point in wasting valuable time looking for a needle in a haystack. *Just nail Tattoos for murder and call it a night*, he chuckled.

Aguilar wondered what the actual charges would evolve into with this one. It was certainly an anomaly with the presence of the boiled bodies and the missing brown kid, but it all came right back to these people tossing their kind across a desert as cruel as this one. Same shit, different day. As he left his office and turned off the lights, the report on the case was tossed in a pile with about 46 others.

It would sit there for a while.

CHATTY CHUMP

There was a new cut on Bozo. That made four now all across the light brown plush, always appearing on Mondays after Judith left Sarah alone for a few hours the day before to run errands. The cuts were easy to count since Judith had made a point to sew him back together with black thread so the cuts would *really* show. *Things don't go back to the way they were.* That's what she hoped Sarah would learn, hoped a lesson could be made out of this, as she always hoped. She was hoping every moment was a parenting moment, hypervigilant over her mannerisms, her approaches, all of them steeped in this moralizing tone, to make a fable out of every significant moment she spent with her daughter. Maybe it was more for herself than for Sarah, she admitted. Maybe it was to make herself feel like she really was trying to be a parent.

She unfolded the stepladder to reach the old cookie tin filled with sewing supplies above the kitchen cupboard, and she thought of how stupid her lesson really was. Sarah had said she would never do it again three times now, each time swearing and tearing up until she was out of breath, and yet here was Bozo, his warped grin and beady plastic eyes, hardly looking like the happy, spotless sloth it had come out of the box as, and more like a fuzzy Frankenstein's monster, speckled in dried-up, gray chewing gum and missing tufts of hair here and there, a big tear just above his dangly, rope-like right leg.

Maybe there's no point, Judith thought while working the needle, the two-inch cut now only a tenth of its size, the thread closing the window through which the sloth's white cotton insides could be seen. The stitchwork with the light-brown thread left no trace of any violation. She had decided to just give it up. There was no point in leaving the thing looking like a zombie. She chuckled, seeing Bozo's ever-present smile, even as she worked the sharp needle in and out of him. *You're one tough cookie*, she decided, and maybe that's what Sarah needed: A tough friend that could take the brunt of whatever possessed her daughter to be so cruel to the poor little thing.

Once she was done, she picked the animal up with both hands like a small child and wondered how to work it. She pressed around his long arms, his head, until she finally found some hard plastic device inside his tummy, like pushing through the softness of skin to find bone. She pressed it, feeling some kind of button give beneath her thumb, which activated Bozo's voice box.

"*Please don't!*" Bozo answered to her touch, the tinny, muffled voice still recognizably Sarah's, but sounding afraid.

Chatty Chumps, they were called. There was a sloth, a dog, a cow, maybe a frog, Judith seemed to recall, each with a built-in microphone and speaker. "Make your Chump chat with you!" "2GB of audio storage!" "Make them say anything!" "Wireless charging!" The writing around the obnoxiously colored box was coming back to her in flashes as she pressed again.

"*It hurts! Please stop!*" Bozo said this time, Sarah's voice breaking as if something was really hurting. It did not sound like a game a child would play.

Sarah had begged so much, even thrown a tantrum in the middle of dinner, which she never did, for one of these things. Not that it would necessarily break the bank, but Judith had thought there was no point when there were so many other lovelier dolls and plushies at goodwills and flea markets—nothing a little laundry soap couldn't fix. Finally, she had given in during one of those moments of relentless adoration that came with her weakness, at full force, deplorably so, as any parenting guide would condemn them.

"Of course I'll get you one," she had said to Sarah between mouthfuls of ice cream. The look of joy in her daughter's eyes was a burning that Judith loved to warm up against, smearing a small bit of vanilla on her nose. "You look like a clown!" She had said, both of them giggling like two little girls exchanging secrets, indulging in their mutual carelessness, in their mutual need to feel unbridled, irresponsible love. Later they had driven to the nearest department store, and Sarah picked out Bozo almost at random, as if it was not the actual toy she was ecstatic to have, but rather just the feeling of grabbing it and tearing it out of the box.

And now this.

She pressed it a third time. "*You're killing me! You're killing me!*" It was Sarah alright, making her best impression of agony, of moments before a fatal attack, an emotion she could not possibly have a frame of reference for. Judith could hear the stifled innocence in her voice even through the cheaply made speaker.

She threw the sloth on the couch and made her way to Sarah's room, running hands through drawers, through socks and underwear and soft blouses, through pastel-colored linen and covers and under pillows, trying to find the coldness of a sharp blade to lay the blame on. The closest she found were some blunt arts-and-crafts scissors for kids that couldn't even stab through paper unless one really tried. Of course, it wouldn't have been hard to grab a knife from the kitchen, but would Sarah really disobey her so after countless warnings to stay away from the kitchen drawers? *Well, there's Bozo with a huge gash even after she said she'd stop.*

Judith went through every knife in every drawer, eyeing each blade carefully with her sewing glasses on, trying to find the smallest bit of incriminating fabric lodged in a serrated edge, telling herself, *Of course the cuts were too clean to be an accident. What kind of playing around would make that cut? It wouldn't have been this big knife, or this little one either, if it was just a clean stab.* Mechanically, she ran through this cold reasoning, putting the "why" away, putting the nauseating fizzle of her panic away, cramming it down in her gut, swallowing hard. In busying her hands she ignored the broader questions, the devastating nature of the implications, of hearing Bozo echo those words back to her, words of pain, torture, and something broader and crueler and more perverse arresting her daughter's mind. None of it mixed with Sarah, angel-faced and often scruffy from playground hijinks, her broad smile missing two lower teeth, beaming all the time.

Baby, my baby, she wouldn't do that. Oh, baby, baby. She cradled that word in her mind while examining knives.

Then she heard the school bus pull up to the front of her house, then tiny footsteps growing louder and louder as they approached the front door. By the time the door flung opened, there was no evidence of any of the previous maddened searching, only Judith sitting with Bozo on the sofa.

"Mom! Mom!" chimed in the high-pitched voice as Judith felt a small embrace wrap itself around her hips. A hand instinctively went down to caress Sarah's hair as the child buried her face into her mother's jeans. Fingers caked in green watercolors turned a pinkish red as they locked tight around Judith and refused to let go.

Judith began to say something, but the kid unwrapped herself from her and made her way to her room to drop off her backpack and jacket. Judith fiddled with the stuffed toy, as if searching for answers in the thin and short felt, like there might be something inscribed in braille on the brown fabric, a last-minute *a-ha*—but nothing. How was she to even approach the matter when she wasn't even sure what the matter was? There had been no time to consider anything, only that icy and wrinkled pain in her gut when she tried thinking of these overwhelming questions: *Why would she do something so strange? Why does she keep disobeying? Why would she grab a knife?*

Sarah retraced her steps and was back next to Judith, who still hadn't managed a single word. The little girl's eyes fixed intently on Bozo.

"Bozo ripped again, mom," she said in a softer voice now, her flushed cheeks slowly cooling back down to a pale, visibly nervous countenance. "I meant to tell you."

"I know," Judith said. "He did, didn't he? But I fixed him, see?"

Sarah smiled softly, a smile that surely hid something. This could not escape Judith's gaze. "Can I have him?" She asked carefully.

As if the toy had never meant a thing to Judith, at once it was back in Sarah's hands, and the little girl marched off to her bedroom. It had slipped from Judith's grip, easy as water, with a myriad of thoughts thumping around her head that would never find a way out.

While Sarah played in her room, Judith searched her mind for some comforting logic. She recalled herself most of all, Sarah's age, in those long nights while her dad worked the casino nightshifts, and her mom was nowhere to be seen for 5 years. She recalled nude baby dolls obscenely posed on their headless necks, a grotesque display of flesh-colored plastic. She recalled Barbies burned with dad's lighters, tossed with force, her vicious puppeteering reeling them into all manner of tasteless scenarios: broken marriages and domestic tragedies with Ken, crude murder scenes, or just a relentless and looping suicide, the same skinny, nude doll diving headfirst from the vast cliff that was the edge of her bed, only to be brought back up by an idle hand that would force her to self-destruction all over again. All of Judith's dolls had always been nude, all carefully inspected, as if the phantom of a nipple or a vulva would one day reveal itself carefully hidden in that insincere plastic skin, leading to the defogging of fleshly secrets Judith hadn't even understood at all at that age. *These are just the games children play*, she told herself, even though earlier this had not made sense. Then, she added, *Or maybe just* some *children, the ones that are more* broken.

So, as Bozo had left her hand, she had decided that's what it was: Sarah, broken, living with a single mom, shy and insecure and erratic around toys, *that* girl, like her mom and her fucked-up Barbies, and with her burn-out dad long gone. This stung, but it didn't chill and constrict the way all other shapeless possibilities had when they had been spinning in her head. In that brief remembrance of Joseph, her ex-husband, she began seething, the faint memory of every corner of that home reeking of alcohol coming back to haunt her. She was not entirely convinced that she should find any more comfort in the possibility that her daughter was just as frustrated as she had been with her broken family and odd childhood. She did, however, find comfort in thinking, *So* that's *what it is, and we can manage it. We can start looking for solutions.*

...And I turned out alright, she thought to herself while putting the sewing supplies away, a bit in jest at the sound of such a trite parental statement, but still, she really saw the truth in it. Not even working full-time, but still the shining bright Seller of the Month at her real estate office,

she had gotten them both a home, with all the comforts and amenities intact, a home that was sparsely decorated, but bright and welcoming enough to have guests feeling at ease while admiring it. Most importantly, she had spare money enough to buy useless things like Bozo, and time enough to be there for her daughter, to be back home early enough to find the toy sloth in a scene that perhaps a true, full-time parent was never meant to see, a little slip on the child's part. It was the way children do many things in secret: In the liminal spaces of working hours while parents are away, things adults are never to witness, playing games that are to only remain in the child's private memories. At least Judith knew there were things *she* had done in childhood that she would take unspoken to her grave.

She resettled back into the couch, trying to read but not absorbing anything. *Therapy*. That was the word thumping and glowing now and then with a soft, uncomfortable burning. She certainly could afford it, had the time and money. It would do Sarah wonders, many experts would say, but how did one even get a therapist, and one for an eight-year-old girl at that? *I can find out*. And she would. Still, the burning persisted, and she caught herself with a sorrowful indignance at acknowledging that the burning was *shame*. She had been defeated in some way, she felt, knowing Joseph really had done something long-lasting, something that needed remedying when he had just disappeared without warning, easy as that. Easy for *him*, but now Judith knew his grime wasn't going to be scrubbed away so easily. Now Sarah needed *therapy*.

But for what? Judith argued with herself, at once tossing the book aside. No reading would get done. *For what exactly? For stabbing a toy sloth.* Was she jumping ahead? Therapy would surprise them all: the teachers, the other parents, shit, it was surprising *her* then just thinking about it. Sarah was a straight-A student, a bright and kind young girl, a bit awkward, but no one ever complained of any worrying signs. These were the reasons why she had even hesitated to jump to conclusions about the toy scenario: Sarah was *not* aggressive.

So, Judith would give it time. She would ask around, softly, approach the subject with caution, maybe at a parent-teacher conference, suggest some interest in therapy, only to see if it was truly needed, and what it would even do. She wasn't even sure what the fuck therapy was. Just talking it out with some rando shrink? Pills? *She* had never needed therapy. She had never needed it, and she turned out alright.

So had Sarah, she knew, so quiet, as if not even in her room, playing with Bozo. She wondered how they played at that very moment. Then, Judith laughed at herself because at that moment she hated Bozo. *All your fucking fault*, she should've said to him. *I never should have found you all ripped up. Why did I press that fucking button?* Maybe Bozo deserved to get stabbed. Maybe next time she'd just let him fall apart, wishing she had a dog that could chew it up to bits.

Judith then remembered that soon after Bozo came home, there had been brief but insistent talk of a dog on Sarah's part, maybe prying to see if that moment of indulgence was still open to more suggestion, but Judith had regained composure. She had said, "Not now, not for a while," to a dog. Then, she imagined Sarah sneaking to the kitchen to grab that same knife she had used to cut up Bozo, and how that knife would reveal insides more wondrous and bountiful than what Bozo hid under its fake pelt, and then she thought of how a dog would not need to be told through a microphone how and what to squeal when stabbed.

So, Judith said to herself that therapy it would be.

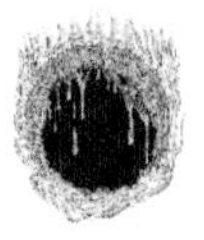

Sarah didn't know how to make Bozo stop.

"D-dick-licking c-c-cunt," he said back to her in her own voice, stuttering and a bit unsure, words she had never even uttered, words she had trouble with the meaning of, but that still, with their inflection and their sonic shape, had all the bricklike weight of being dirty, dirty words.

"Bozo," she whispered to him, voice shaking. She was terrified. Even though Sarah knew full well the sloth couldn't see out of his plastic eyes, in this unfolding of something so cruel and senseless, like reality was a veil being lifted within the privacy of her bedroom (as in the moment of all her games), she did not want him to *see* her cry. She thought he really could. She was pressing the "Stop" button on the remote control he had come with, over and over, to no avail. "Bozo, you need to stop."

"Bitch," he said. That one she knew. "Fuck you." Another one she knew. "Stupid cunt." The words were fractured, with the hesitation of someone not fully in control of such adult crassness. It was profane glossolalia, almost comical coming from such a small speaker under the tiny, fuzzy body, something its circuits and voice coil were never meant to project.

"Bozo!" she raised her voice, surprised at her own courage. "Bozo, shut up!"

Bozo tried to scream over her voice, saying the same two words over and over. "STUPID CUNT."

She looked out the window, making sure mom's car still wasn't in the driveway. It was always when she went off on Sundays and left her alone that Bozo would start, like Bozo knew who was and wasn't there. She didn't want mom to hear, but Bozo showed no signs of stopping.

"Bozo, shut up! Mom's gonna hear!"

"I know you like it," Bozo said, the voice still like Sarah's, but somehow frosted over, almost imperceptibly dropping an octave or two, the words now trickling out rather than coming with stabbing force. "I know you liked to do it. I know you loved it."

She tried the remote again, but nothing changed. Sarah then ran to the kitchen, and even from there she heard Bozo, now screaming his furious accusations, a volume the built-in speakers surely couldn't reach on their own. The voice felt echoing, gnarled and clipped, and like it made a dozen few cuts every time Sarah felt them enter her ears. "YOU BITCH! YOU FUCKING BITCH! I KNOW YOU LIKED THE LICKING HE GAVE YOU!"

She reached for the same knife she always went for, the middle-sized one mom always left near the sink. Running back, she felt fear still dancing around in her throat, but with the knife gripped tight, she also felt some of the fear bubbling up to her head with anger, with resolve, with a need to hurt. She knew Bozo didn't like the knife.

"If you don't stop I'll kill you!" she yelled at the toy once back in her room. "And I mean it this time! I'm gonna chop your head off!"

"No, don't!" pleaded Bozo, the change of voice instantaneous. The gnarled fury cooled into a pleading whimpering, but one that had long since stopped working on Sarah. She knew Bozo was a liar, and that was his liar voice.

"Don't hurt me! Please!" Bozo cried again after Sarah said nothing, using Sarah's own voice. It echoed back with an even bigger fear than the one she felt, as if she were begging to herself, begging not to feel any more of this confused and dulling pain that the girl and the toy always exchanged when alone.

"Stop saying things like that then!" she yelled back, angry at herself for falling for him again. "Just be nice and stop saying—"

"YOUR DADDY!" Bright red, blistering words like boiling water splashing against her face.

"Bozo, stop! You—"

"YOUR DADDY PUT HIS TONGUE—"

No more arguing was done at that point, just screaming and crying from Sarah's worn throat.

"REMEMBER HE SAID MY LITTLE BABY WATCH THE TONGUE GO UP AND DOWN. GO ON AND TELL DADDY WHERE YOU WANT THE TONGUE. UP AND DOWN. REMEMBER DADDY SAID WATCH IT GO UP AND DOWN—"

The stabbing, as always, felt like digging into sand, her tiny, shaking fist working the blade deep inside Bozo, past the curls of cotton, like the fibrous tearing of some make-believe muscle. It froze his voice for a moment as the two were engaged in this contact, in this impossible balance between a game and a real murder.

"Shut up!" she screamed, although all was quiet.

"Please stop!" Bozo wailed back in Sarah's voice, the rattling onset of crying fully heard in his wire throat, though the small thing had no tears to shed. "You're hurting me! It hurts! Please stop!"

"*SHUT UP!*" Sarah screamed back at the top of her lungs, so unbearably loud it made her entire body flush with heat and shaking. She was trying her best to believe the little thing was hurt, but she knew it was not.

Bozo was quiet then. Sarah removed the knife, and for some reason she still curiously eyed the insides of the sloth through the new cut just under his neck. Dull whiteness greeted her, dry the way a stab shouldn't be, leaving behind no seeping pain, but simply the rough impression that hurt had been intended, and that fury had somewhat been quenched. Sarah then stabbed and cut three more times in quick succession, widening the cut until Bozo's head was nearly off. She tossed him under the bed, then sat in a corner of her room, hugging her legs close to her body.

Mom would be home any time, but in that brief stillness in that empty house that was entirely her own for just those few hours, she sat in silence.

Then, she thought of all that Bozo had said.

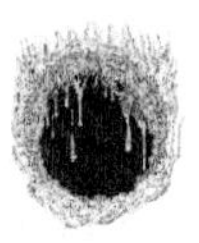

"Sarah, what's wrong?" Judith asked. It was the question she wanted the answer to the most, yet she immediately regretted asking it, knowing it would just give Sarah an easy way to avoid it. *When has that question ever worked?* she scolded herself while digging out cake crumbs and sticky sweet frosting from between her teeth. Her tongue danced around in frustration, trying to find more useful words. The rest of the cake was at the table, round and yellow with no writing, just an impromptu cake for no occasion, already missing two slices. Sarah had eaten hers heartily.

"Nothing, mommy," Sarah answered as expected, with a soft and unbothered voice, eyeing the cake eagerly, ready for seconds whenever they might be offered. She gently patted a napkin around her lips, the perfect likeness to a proper young lady from the movies.

Judith would oblige, of course, and give her daughter as much cake as she wanted. She still believed that in all the unbridled and smothering pampering, Sarah would find the comfort she needed to loosen her voice, like the right words had to be aggressively tickled out of her. *We really need to talk.* This she knew, although she did not have the first clue as to how they would get there. She knew they had to talk as mother and daughter, though now she sat at the table looking like another little girl invited to the tea party, nervous and indulging in her own spoiling treats, suddenly feeling a random flush of embarrassment. *Some mother...*

"Are you sure?" she insisted, and for the first time since they had sat down to have the pizza dinner and surprise desert, Judith's eyes darted over to Bozo sitting between them, propped up on a chair of his own. His head was sewn back on, a long, dark line circling his neck, the bold suture a loud accusation which Judith had reinstalled, and which Sarah still ignored. "Do you wanna tell me what happened to Bozo?" She surprised herself with such a forward question, but since she had discovered the tattered thing under Sarah's bed, she had *needed* to know. He had been nearly decapitated, the tears frayed and uneven like they had not been before, this time marked by an explosive anger that seemed to have come into that home from nowhere, an anger that couldn't exist anywhere between her and Sarah, that sweet young girl eating her cake.

"He had an accident," Sarah answered without missing a beat.

"Sarah," Judith said with added sternness (or at least she hoped so), sighing loudly, parsing through the possible words to say. The little girl wasn't going to give in. Perhaps this, too, was a game to her, and Judith was desperate for a way to make it known that it wasn't. "Sarah, why did you cut Bozo's head off? You can tell me, honey." That was the best she could manage, desperately clutching for the words of child psychologists and parenting experts like scripture, things she half-remembered reading about "Communication":

1. *Make it known that there's a problem that needs resolving.*
2. *Be respectful but confrontational.*
3. *Assert authority but be kind and open.*

Fucking easy for them to say, she thought, exasperated. The sweetness in her mouth from the cake was now turning sour, uncomfortable. It dawned on her that this was not a moment to be eating cake, and her embarrassment swelled even more.

"I didn't, mommy!" Sarah shouted back, still at a sensible volume, but with obvious indignance. "I didn't! I told you he had an accident!"

"Okay, then what was the accident? How did Bozo manage to tear his head off all on his own?"

"I don't know, mommy!"

"How do you not know? Aren't you with Bozo all the time?"

"Sometimes he hides!"

They were back in the game. *Make it known it's not a game. Don't play into it.* This made it sound like warfare, like she needed to fight her own daughter. She *hated* that. How could she even manage to untangle this frustration when she herself had made everything seem like it *was* indeed a game? From the moment she had initiated the "confrontation," everything went the way of cakes and pizza and sitting Bozo at the table without a single reprimand. Sarah hadn't even blinked when Judith first showed her the reassembled toy. *Pathetic, fucking pathetic mother.* For a moment, she realized there was bile rising in her throat, realized that maybe all the sweets and treats had been also for *her*, to cushion herself, sit herself at a table she wanted to sit at, and not confront whatever ugliness was now haunting her daughter and this toy. Maybe Judith also wanted this to just be a game. Then, the most she could think to do was be sincere about her suspicions, however revolting they were.

"Is this about your dad, honey? Are you angry?"

Silence. *That* had definitely changed the mood. Sarah's face froze, her tiny frame falling back into her chair from which she had risen to echo her retorts.

"Are you angry at daddy, Sarah?" Judith asked again, feeling her own anger, her own repulsion and sadness bubbling up, burning her throat as she said such clinical, biting words. These were words she only ever pieced together to ball them up and never utter. They were coarse. They hurt to pass. "Is this about—"

"Bozo had an accident, mom," Sarah said again, receding into a cooing little voice, softer, higher.

It was a distant voice now only reserved to memory. Instantly upon hearing it, it flared up baby talcum into Judith's nostrils. Yes, it was baby talcum, Marigold shampoo, plastic nipples washed in boiling water, Sarah as a tiny thing, barely bigger than Bozo, crawling around the house in a jangle of rattles and teething toys. That was the Sarah she heard now, answering back, as if that little Sarah, so precious and sacred, had returned, leaving the enigmatic, hard-to-deal-with Sarah behind.

"Sarah, I've been thinking about therapy, honey," Judith stated as if to regain her composure. She swallowed hard, unable to look her own daughter in the eyes. "I don't know what's going on, but I think the way you're treating Bozo is a bit concerning... I've told you over and over to take care of him, and you disobey, and the way he gets torn up tells me that..." *That what?* She ran out of words just then. She had managed to circle back to therapy, which she couldn't believe. The talking points in her head, once ordered so neatly as she had rehearsed them on her own, now lay scattered in an empty vastness, words like stepping stones, and she was trying to reach each one, but the gaps were widening. Still, she had managed to arrive at that big one, "Therapy," but now she did not know what to do once there, and Sarah's soft baby voice was crawling back with the same sickly sweetness as the cake in her throat.

"Mom," the little girl almost babbled, "can I go play with Bozo?"

Yes! She wanted to scream. *Just go play with Bozo!* "Not yet, honey," she forced herself to say. "We're still talking."

Then, they sat in silence for a while. Judith offered another slice of cake, and Sarah took it with beaming eyes. The little girl ate, her eyes now focused intently on the toy sloth, Judith only nibbling away at some pizza crust.

With enough time, Judith rephrased it all in her mind like coiling spilled guts in her fingers and reeling them back in, not with any neatness, but in a shape that retained some kind of order. *We went over this already, girl. Little kids break their toys all the time. Brenda at the office is always complaining that her children are slowly tearing her house apart, stripping off bits of wallpaper and tearing holes in couches. Sarah is tearing up her toys, and what are toys for anyway? Shit, don't they even sell little punching bags and stress things to squeeze and bite and all that stuff? Maybe I'm just angry that she chose the most expensive one to behead.* She almost smiled. Of course, it was so silly now to think about. *Therapy? Really, Judith? Over a torn-up sloth? Let the poor girl shred it to bits in peace. You're lucky she's not tearing the mattress apart or something*. Still, she would ask someone, anyone with kids, how normal it was. Not quite therapy, but she would *ask*. It was a start. This thought comforted her, and she stayed there a while with quiet pleasure at her proposed solution.

I will ask. It was like a lifesaver, a warm ray of sunshine. *I'll start by just asking. I will ask*.

"Are you sure there's nothing else you want to tell me, honey?" Judith asked one more time, but it may as well have been her saying goodbye.

Sarah smiled, knowing exactly what Judith wanted to hear, knowing that she had helped her mother dig herself out of an uncomfortable pit. She knew what words felt like release to mom. The conversation, it seemed, had only been to calm Judith and Judith alone, with Sarah holding full authority over how to pamper and comply and dissuade her mom's suspicions.

"No, mommy," she answered.

"Alright, just one more thing, then," Judith said, grabbing Bozo from his chair. "Please, please, *please*, little lady, take care of poor Bozo, okay?"

"Yes, mommy. I'm sorry." And there it was: That was the first time Sarah had apologized, as good as any admittance of guilt. She was no longer playing at Bozo hurting himself. Her mistake, her apology. *A lesson had been learned.*

Judith smiled in reply, and out of curiosity, before handing him over, she thought to search for that switch under the membrane of fur that made Bozo talk. She found the give of the button and pressed it.

Nothing but Sarah's exaggerated sounds of snoring through the roughed-up voice box answered: "Ha-choo, ha-choo."

Sarah giggled. "Cause he's a sloth!" she said. "All he does is sleep!"

Judith laughed, too, and handed the toy over.

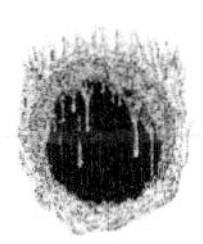

Sarah was shut in the closet. Bozo had not stopped for what seemed like hours. She was sure mom would be back any second, but she had promised. *I'm not gonna hurt Bozo anymore.*

The words came clear, no longer tinny or garbled. They were solid words pounding in that room with her, strung not by wires and coils but by vocal cords alive with hot and angry breath. "IN THE DIAPERS. IN THE DIAPERS. IN THE DIAPERS."

Sarah clutched the knife tightly, her small hand a bright red knob in the dark, trembling. She had not realized when her laughter had turned to crying. They had started playing "Telling Secrets," as always. Sarah had hit record and told Bozo what to say. "Mom talks too loud," she had blurted out at first, giggling at herself, deciding to hit delete afterward just to be safe. "Mrs. Bronson smells like pee." This one had made her cackle. "Laura is so ugly." "I hate how Rosie makes weird noises in class."

And then Bozo had started again with his own contribution. "Sarah is so dumb," he said with Sarah's own voice, borrowing it again on his own. Sarah had laughed at the stupid, ever-present smile on the dumb sloth.

"*You're* dumb!" she had countered, initiating their sneery, childish arguing. "Your name is *Bozo*, you bozo!"

However, it had then started to be very nervous laughter coming from her. It was the way a child laughs after flying off a swing or scraping a knee, looking around for adults and their faces, to see if they had horror or joy in their eyes, instructing on how to react. There, however, in the solitude of her and Bozo's games, there were never adults, and so she had simply sunk into her own confusion. "Sarah is so ugly." "Sarah is shit." "Sarah eats shit." "Sarah eats shit." Bozo had gone on and on. Sarah had felt like gluing her tear ducts shut, hoping the anger and fear would get gulped down soon, and she had kept laughing.

"Shut up!" she had yelled once but she couldn't take it anymore, for Bozo yelling ugly words on his own had just grown too monstrous again, too weird to be just a game. She had recalled Bobby, the gap-toothed kid from the previous schoolyear, touching her thigh while playing doctor, recalled how her smile faded even though his didn't, and recalled punching him square on the nose once she knew that was *not* how games were played. Bozo's games always felt the same as Bobby's hand, so she had twisted the poor toy's arms behind his back, hoping that even in its cotton guts there would be at least a single nerve that would ache. At this, she had laughed again. She didn't know how to do much else whenever her playtime would unwind into this tense back-and-forth. Every time, Bozo started with something slow and hurtful, as if easing her into the aggression to follow. She hated how his smile never left.

Now she cried. Now it *really* wasn't a game. Now she was in the closet, legs close to her body, and Bozo was talking, at a sensible level now, about his things.

"You saw when he went into the diapers—"

She tried to scream for him to stop but her voice had given out. She looked down at her hands. They trembled, still red from her tight grip on the knife, and cold, and she felt hot vomit swish in her belly, spaghetti and tomato sauce mixing with something bitter that felt like it had been in there a long time.

"You saw! YOU SAW!" Bozo's voice was still hers somewhat, but more a voice she knew she could use, but never had—rising, impossibly loud. It was angry, but not "I can't find my crayons" angry, not "I stubbed my toe" angry. It was an anger that felt like another person was sitting in the middle of her room, ready to do hurtful, unbearable things to her.

The closet door opened slowly. A shy pair of eyes peeked out, searching for the source of all the chatter, searching where the laughter was now falling from, thick and bitter.

"YOU SAW HIM!"

A few steps forward, and then a pink-sleeved arm wiped vomit from small, chapped lips crowned in snot. She knew mom would be angry to find the mess in the closet.

"YOU SAW HIM GO THROUGH THE DIAPERS!" Louder now, followed by more strange laughter.

The knife was unsteady. It danced left and right, her knuckles twitching as she tried to tighten her sweaty grasp on the handle.

Bozo was screaming a scream born of flesh, of wind pressing through drool and muscle. "WHEN HE WENT

THROUGH YOUR BABY DIAPERS AND HE SMELLED—"

"SHUT UP!" Sarah managed to scream again. "SHUT UP! SHUT UP! SHUT UP!"

"WHEN HE WENT THROUGH YOUR BABY DIAPERS," the same angry screaming voice answered back. "AND SAID HE SMELLED THEM SAID HE SMELLED THEM BECAUSE THEY SMELLED LIKE YOU DOWN THERE HE SAID HE WENT AND SMELLED YOUR DIAPERS AND PULLED IT OUT—"

The knife lunged forward.

"PULLED IT OUT AND THREW THE WHITE STUFF ON YOUR DIAPERS BECAUSE THEY SMELLED LIKE YOU DOWN THERE HE SAID—"

She felt the knife tear through the cloth and cotton, felt it go deep into something solid and plastic, something very much like a rock-hard lung from which words still kept screaming even as the sharp point of the blade labored to undo them.

"HE PULLED HIS THING OUT AND THREW THE WHITE STUFF ON YOUR DIAPERS BECAUSE THEY SMELLED LIKE YOU DOWN THERE THEY SMELLED LIKE YOU DOWN THERE—"

Then Sarah started laughing when Bozo said nothing more, feeling the knife crush the wiring that kept the hideous voice alive. She felt the voice box give its last whimper before falling into a deep gurgle. She kept stabbing, her voice now the one rising above everything else. Bozo, face and tummy undone, still watched with glass eyes fixed forever on her twisting face.

"HE PULLED HIS THING OUT!" Sarah's voice resounded, even if Bozo's voice box was destroyed down to the last wire. Yet, it still sounded very much like it came from Bozo, sounding very much like Sarah, jumping up and down the throat with feigned exaltation, with histrionic pain, the way a child would have a toy soldier bewail its last moments. "HE PULLED HIS THING OUT AND HE DID IT ON THE DIAPERS!"

The stabbing persisted, the knife being loosely flung this way and that. Sometimes it fell on Bozo, others on the duvet covers, the bleeding fuzzy white cotton flying everywhere.

"SHUT UP!" Sarah said. Bozo was still very much talking, she decided. He was very much still yelling his things.

"AND WHEN HE WAS DONE WITH THE DIAPERS—" again it was Bozo with Sarah's voice.

And now the knife started cutting small, white fingers and making them go red. The sharp thing still stood cradled in Sarah's hands, but Sarah's hands were now fuzzy and brown, long black claws curled firmly around the handle, the red now dripping on the white duvet. Then they were Sarah's hands again stabbing at Bozo.

"HE WENT TO GO AND SMELL YOU AND—"

The tip of the knife still hungrily searched for where that noise was coming from. The voice was now all over the room, and that's where the knife went, here and there, somewhere invisible between Bozo and Sarah who were locked in a vicious conversation. The knife flew and pecked around and searched some more until it felt the low vibration of real human words wrapped in the soft flesh of her neck.

"HE SAID NOW I WANNA SMELL YOUR THING NOW I WANNA LICK YOUR THING NOW I WANNA SMELL THE REAL THING—"

And it felt the soft, fuzzy wrappings of her throat peel back layer by layer and the red fell on the white duvet.

"NOW I WANNA SMELL AND LICK AND FEEL THE REAL THING—"

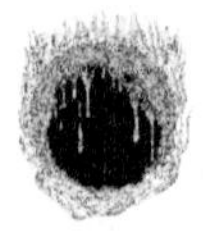

Judith came back to a quiet house. She had been thinking about Sarah and their previous conversation, the soothing of her previous conclusions no longer sitting right. She was exhausted from going back and forth on the matter. She had managed to ask Brenda, and it had all come pouring out in shameful crying in the break room. Brenda had reassured her there was nothing wrong with Sarah, and that they needed to just talk. It felt like just polite half-advice, but Judith had cherished it.

"But if the toy really bothers you," Brenda had said. "Do what I do with my kids' toys. When they get their hands on a really noisy, annoying one, I just throw it away and pretend I know nothing."

Judith had laughed but decided she would do just that. $40 in the trash were better than the little fuzzy fuck making her go insane.

"Sarah?" she called out but received no answer. She hurled her keys and coat on the sofa and went to inspect. Sarah was always eager to receive her on Sundays when she returned—and now she knew it was probably after shuffling to hide a torn Bozo somewhere. She wondered if this was what her daughter was busy with at that moment. Would she finally catch her daughter red-handed? *Would she really, after promising not to do it again? But Brenda said it sounded normal to her. It sounds like a kid playing. Still, if she disobeyed, we need to talk*. They would talk, she thought over and over. They would really talk if this was the case.

"Sarah, what are you up to?" she called out after knocking on the pink bedroom door. She recalled when they had painted that, soon after Joseph had left. She felt stupid once more, how she thought mother and daughter hurling paint around would be enough distraction. Now the door stood between her and whatever strange games her daughter played behind it. "Can I come in?" she cautioned once more before opening it.

As it flung open, the distinct smell of child's vomit hit her nose, the unmistakable half-digested school lunch and tomato sauce she had dealt with countless times before. Her gaze at first only met the bedroom window, showing the park across the road where children enjoyed their Sunday afternoon. As she lowered her eyes to continue her search, she found Sarah, face-down, where the soft blue carpet had turned red.

Judith had countless thoughts flash through her mind as she stumbled around the child's room, nearly fainting. The room seemed to spin and spin like the foundation of the house was a teacup seat at a carousel, flashes of green and red carnival lights, the old but familiar scent of deep-fried carnival food reaching her from a distant corner of her mind, mixing with the reek of child vomit, mixing with the reek of her own vomit now clashing yellowish and green against the already stained soft blue carpet. Her legs tried to go to the child, but they bent this way and that, still searching for steadiness in the relentless carnival spin—the carnival teacup ride she and Joseph had ridden when they first met, when she went with him even though her friend Paula had said that he gave her the creeps. That's where that memory came from. It had been the same night the little thing known as Sarah had been conceived, the thing that rushed them to that ugly, ugly marriage.

But now there was the little thing known as Sarah, a bundle of wet red lying perfectly still, stiller than sleep. Without having touched her, Judith knew she was cold. She could see it in those white pebble-like hands. But they needed to talk. That's what she remembered as she managed to gain some shaky footing and stumbled towards her daughter. They needed to talk because Judith would finally find the right words. She would finally get to talk about what was going on when she was gone, what weird things swept through that house when she was not there. *I need you to talk to me, sweetie*, she said in her head just as she had been rehearsing the phrase the entire time she was running errands, but now she could only say it to herself, not even managing to get it out so her daughter could hear, though she knew words, as firm as they might emerge this time around, would now only swirl like soundless spit around the hole of her ear.

Judith never noticed when she started holding Sarah in her arms. From one second to the other, she was there, cradling her little girl, her sweater soaked, nothing left unstained except the open eyes fixed right on her, but not seeing her, seeing only something dark and heavy beyond her face, beyond the ceiling, the mouth festooned with red, oily strings the same red color as everything else on that one spot where she had fallen. *The strings... coming from her throat...* Judith saw how they were cut and mangled, but then she looked up and shut her eyes tight and saw and said no more.

She never noticed that she had stepped on Bozo on her way to her daughter, He had been in the way, discarded on the floor, arms and legs this way and that, cotton filling gutted out like little clouds. She never noticed when her heel pressed down the button, activating the voice box, low and wilted final sounds coming from the cut wires:

"Ha-choo, ha-choo," the little sloth snored.

DIRTY WATER

There were broken bottles in the deeper part of the canal that could cut your feet. I remember once seeing Itza try to skate across the water, then lots of red bubbling up, and then her screaming as we all ran off laughing, because of course she should have known better. Everyone knew the canal could cut up your feet in the deeper part, so you never planted your feet down, and everyone knew you never swam past the dry tree with its branches arching over the dirty water.

We all laughed at Itza for doing something so reckless, but here I was now, my feet only inches away from the sharp glass, trying to seem calm but always aware of where my feet were floating, doing a panicked kick every few seconds to keep myself afloat, because Yaya and Nena had said that I was too much of a baby to swim past the arch of branches. They had said it just to say it, I know, offhand and soft while brushing their dolls' broken hairs, knowing it would get me going. Indeed, without a stutter, I kicked my chanclas off and said I would.

Being inside the water, however, so close to shredding my feet like that dumb girl Itza, so close to the arch of branches, I was starting to think maybe I *was* too baby. I had never been so close to the tree arch while inside the water. By land on the banks of the canal, where one could pass the tree by foot with no issue (it was swimming through the branches that was trouble), it had only looked as tall as maybe Yaya, the tallest of us three, and the branches seemed few and in a high enough arch above the water that they could never really be trouble. Of course, we never got a *really* good look at the tree up close, because no one played near *that* tree. Yet, it had never struck me as an *evil* tree, whatever that looked like. There, however, already in the cold and filthy water, the tree seemed *immense*, like it had grown overnight. The branches were many and all coiled up into limbs that looked like thin bird bones, all insistent on growing downwards, desperate to dive into the water, but never breaking its surface. However, there were some branches near me that almost reached my bobbing head, and others further in I was sure could scratch my scalp if I wasn't careful.

"Mira a la coyona," I heard Nena jeering, her arms folded across her chest. "I knew she was too scared!"

I smiled, and made sure she saw me smile, because I heard the doubt rattle in her voice, seeing me bobbing up and down further in than any of us had ever dared swim, almost past the outer limit of the arch. I didn't see her smiling when she made fun of me, so I knew she didn't mean it. I knew she was just scared because I was actually going to do it. I just had to keep going.

"Keep going!" yelled Yaya, as if knowing what I was thinking. "You're almost there, but you *have* to go through!"

Their bodies looked so tiny and blurry to me just then. They were just short, brown fuzz shifting their feet on land. I knew they were too scared themselves, but I wasn't going to make fun of them for it just then. This had stopped being about them. I had to prove to *myself* that I could be the bravest girl of us three—the one that dared to swim through the arch, coming out unscathed. I imagined with joyous greed the rewards that would follow this display: how I'd always get first dibs on the candies we'd buy putting our money together, how I'd take the lead riding our bicycles around our barrio from hereon, Yaya's height nothing compared to the bravery I was about to show. I had deduced that if I swam fast and in a straight line, deep enough to avoid the pointy branches above and high enough to never touch the broken glass below, in that perfect, steady swim, I would be just fine.

Besides, it was just branches.

Nobody believed that, of course, but, while taking my last breaths before going under, I tried really hard convincing myself. *It's just a dumb old tree.* It's what all the adults would say. With adults at my side, it would have been cake, because adults say and explain things just how they are, and when it's explained, it makes perfect sense. At least *I* knew when my mommy helped me with things, it was like having this constant opening of eyes ("so that's how *that* works," "so that's what *that* is"). With other kids, however, things always get hazy and make the fear start beating around the sides of my head. Kids always have a story for everything, and for this tree and its arching branches, they had decided: It was a witch's tree, a tree that drowned children before eating their dead bodies, bloating them with dirty canal water like birotes dipped in coffee. *It's evil. Nothing good about it. The farther you are from it, the better.* And now I was going against every playground warning. This thought more than any other made me feel crazy, almost dizzy with thinking how I was swimming where no kid ever swam—alone, so alone.

The last thing I saw was Nena and Yaya running off to the other side of the arch (on the bank opposite from which the tree grew, for added safety). In that moment, drawing in that last final breath, I assured myself that I would see them, scared on the other side, their ugly faces wrinkled in worry, still curling their bare feet on the safety of the ground. I would meet them there as a new me, a braver me, drenched in dirty water and standing tall above them, ready to get used to all the new respect this would bring. With these eager thoughts, my body fully submerged, feeling the cold of the water swallow the top of my head as I began swimming forward.

I only let my eyes open a bit underwater at first, and I instantly regretted it. I immediately felt the floating, microscopic bits of trash and filth crawl under my lids and begin stinging. Some of the trash settled there even after my eyes shut again, irritating spots that felt as if all the way deep in my sockets. I managed to catch only a glimpse of all the broken glass lining the floor of the canal, blending with the rocks and looking oddly pretty in submerged reds and greens. When my eyes shut again, I realized I was quickly losing sense of direction, so I swam blindly, feeling for a way that felt like forward. Breaking through the water once more in one long stroke, my body slipped right beyond the arch.

The water all felt the same here—same temperature, same weight around me. Nothing changed, and I smiled to myself as I swam faster, gaining confidence. Suddenly, all the little kid fear seemed dumb to me, shedding from me. I even felt embarrassed having believed in all their stupid lies in the first place, feeling silly as I swam under a tree I had been so scared of. I could not wait until I touched land again, pointing to the tree with a big smile on my face, asking Nena and Yaya, "You're scared of *that*?!"

With my speed steady and my arms full of energy, I trudged forward through the foamy waters.

When I felt the first branch tangle in my hair, I remained calm, knowing that with sharp branches, something like this was bound to happen. It didn't prove anything. My arms abandoned their swimming position as my hands shot up to my hair, trying to get that thin, brittle branch out of the way. I was hooked right into it, though, and somehow my hair had curled and ensnared all along its length. Still fully submerged, only my fingers poking out through the surface now and then, I had to work quickly while I still had air. However, the branch would not undo its grip. Then the air grew less and less, and bubbles erupted from my nose as I felt some panic settle.

Still relatively calm, I decided I'd go up just enough to let my nose breathe air in, still avoiding some of the low branches. It would help me work more patiently at getting my hair uncaught. However, once I kicked my legs under me to emerge, I miscalculated the strength of my kick and my head instead shot up rather than floated out of the water—straight into the arching branches.

I felt the stabs in my scalp like bony fingers digging straight at my skull. I clenched my lips shut, not wanting the other girls to hear me scream. Now it felt like the tree fully had me, stretching my neck upwards as the grip of its limbs held my head in a tangled, wet mess. Kicking my legs, making the water bubble with gray froth, I stayed afloat, my hands now feeling too small and scared for the job of undoing the mess of knots. The stabbing hurt, but the reason I even managed not to scream in the first place was because it did not hurt as much as I imagined being impaled by so many branches would. It was more of a discomfort, but nonetheless I felt the warm blood start to trickle down my scalp, and I knew I was in trouble.

Needing to steady myself, I knew I had to plant my feet on the canal floor. I felt the strength around my legs quickly running out, my knees already worn from the playing and swimming done that afternoon. I shut my eyes tightly, decided that my feet were going to get cut up if I hoped to get out of there alive. Still, I knew I could plant my feet slowly so that the cuts would only be shallow and short. I still had enough calmness for it. Even though I was not going underwater, I held my breath for added steadiness, and after a few more weakening kicks, my feet gently landed atop the broken glass.

I felt my soles open, and the skin slit apart as the sharp, sharp glass dug through my feet. I looked down and saw blood floating up, vivid and staining the already filthy water, and I saw more drops of the red stuff dripping from my forehead. With all the blood, all the dizziness of being tangled up, the panic of some of that murky water burning up my nostrils and down my throat, I decided it was better to keep my eyes shut. Still, the pain was bearable. I could feel the stabbing, the cutting, the pulling from the branches and the bleeding as I kicked my legs about, but the pain was only a slight prickling.

Uselessly struggling with my hair which would never get untied, I felt even more stabbing breaking about my feet, but it didn't feel like the smooth slicing of the sharp glass anymore. Instead, it felt like more of those branches buried in my scalp attacking from beneath, like the arch was a many-toothed mouth closing not just atop me but all about. Eyes still shut, I felt the prickling and stabbing close in, the space where I'd become tangled becoming smaller and smaller and the water feeling more like just more branches half-submerging me.

Not opening my eyes, I said to myself over and over. *Nope, not doing it.*

Then there was no longer air or space around me. Everything was just branches, stabbing through every extremity, up my nose and mouth and curling down into my lungs and throat, everything just arching branches turning me around like a tongue tasting me and passing me through the corners of a tight mouth. I felt the million, billion stabs, but none of them carried pain after a while. I became more entangled and impaled in the sharp edges, and soon, the space my skin and bones occupied saw itself crushed by the mounting pressure of the branches all about me.

I felt it like infinite little scratches and mosquito bites all across my body. I felt the sensation *fully*, my itchy skin being flayed and pulled open, and I felt more warm blood all about like my body was a big open, shivering wound. I had ceased struggling, and instead tried to draw my limbs close to my body, but now everything was being splayed, suctioned and tugged apart like chewed-up gum. The crackling of the branches was now unbearable, but soon they dug through my ears as well, and all was muffled, thumping with great strength, like the tree was really alive.

I felt my bones extend further than they ever had, felt my hand like it was miles and miles away from my body, and my neck unstitched from atop my shoulders as I felt it stretch down along my back. The vapors around the water were heavy with the stink of garbage, and eventually I stopped breathing, too, as more branches clogged up every hole in my head. Not seeing, not smelling, all I had was the hideous sensation as I soon realized the canal was gently pulling me along, still in the right direction towards the other side of the arch.

I figured it would not be long until the arch spit me out on the winning side. What was most important was that I didn't feel pain, and I didn't feel *dead*. Even feeling all the blood and skin rubbed off me with the vicious tugs and scratches of the branches, I felt very much the same, and knew I'd remain in one piece—scratched to all hell, sure, but in one piece—once I crossed. I wondered how Nena and Yaya would react, seeing me all bloodied, all my flesh barely hanging on to my wrists and ankles. I knew they would scream, but I told myself I would try my hardest to tell them I was alright. *I'm alive*, I told myself to tell them. *I'm all torn up, but I'm alive!*

And just as I neared the end of the arch's assault, I felt the warmth of the sun breaking through the tight bundles of tree limbs. Then I felt all the branches dig themselves out from all about me. More curiously than that, however, I felt my skin resettle in place, the impossible elasticity with which it had been stretched slapping back down to my normal-sized, ironed-down frame. Slowly, even those first branches that had tangled in my hair came undone with ease, and then everything around felt open again, receding, spitting me out into the clearness of the other side.

I had done it. In the crazed joy of my victory, feeling my heart (a heart that just seconds ago had fully felt like it had been torn to shreds by branches in my chest) beating warm blood up and down me, I did not even open my eyes. I ran my hands across my arms, feeling no jagged cuts, no skin falling off. I smiled, triumphant, and just as I opened my eyes again and was greeted by the still shining sun and the calm, smudged face of the canal water, I heard Nena yell my name from land.

When I turned, I locked glances with both her and Yaya, both girls staring intently at me before I saw a brief twitch of fear claw across their expressions. Then, their two little bodies tumbled backward and remained still.

Knowing something was definitely wrong, I swam on, never taking my eyes off the bodies now lying still and peaceful on the wild, dry grass along the canal bank. I felt the water grow shallow, then I felt my feet—my unscathed, uncut feet—plant firmly on land as I ran the last few dripping steps towards my friends. There, as I looked at their faces, I saw the fear settled deep into their rock-hard, creased features. With one brief look at me, they had tumbled back, dead from shock. I knew this wasn't a prank. I screamed at them, too afraid to touch them, and they did not flinch or twitch once. The loudness of my screams, my pleas as I bounced from one's name to the other, all fell idly on them. This was not a game.

I know the arch, with its branches and whatever weird touch its sharp ends have, has changed me. I left the bodies behind, not wanting to accept that something could have struck so much fear into those small hearts that they stopped dead in their tracks.

I don't want to know what they saw.

I want my mommy. I'm crying now that I'm stumbling back home across the empty lots just outside the barrio, a big baby, crying and drenched in dirty water, chewed up and spat out by the evil witch arch. Whatever new form those zillion cuts gave me, I must never see it. I just think of Nena and Yaya and their dead, milky eyes and I start running faster, holding my arms as far from my sight as I can. I'm running straight to my mommy, and I dare not even look down just a bit, afraid of catching even just a glimpse, not wanting to see this new skin the canal gave me.

PART 3: BITES

THE GOOSE

The goose came in through the window. Its webbed feet made a wet sound as they slapped down on the windowsill, its wings resettling to its sides after the effort of flying up to the second floor. The flying had looked more like agitated running, its broad wings unused to flight, bleeding feathers like snowflakes, climbing upwards with a brutal, almost desperate effort. Now it was settled right by the open window, as if its entrance had left it in shock, unsure of whether to proceed or not now that it had gotten this far. It stood there perched for a while, and with it wafted in a soft, fresh wind smelling of pine.

Rigo had noticed the bird many times before. Every single day in those last, down-spiraling weeks before his legs had given out and decided to join death early, leaving him bedbound, he had watched it from the window, on his daily treks to and from the windowsill that had made up the entirety of his excursions. The window was always left open to breathe in something other than the hideous disinfectant that perfumed every sterile corner of his hospital room. The bird frolicked outside in constant passion during daylight hours, always looking proud and aggressive. It was a strange term, "frolicked," to describe a bird's behavior, but one only needed to observe the way the bird seemed to almost *skip* with rabid glee as it chased nearby picknickers or raised its curved wings and stomped around its realm in defiance of whoever. No other word would be as accurate. Rigo had taken an almost faint liking to the thing (*faint*, as all things in those final days were), watching it act out its innermost rages—primitive, vicious, uncaring of whatever other being on Earth may have evolved to the point of easily overpowering it. Rigo recalled reading about birds being the last dinosaurs, the avian kind that persevered through a mass extinction and were now living proof of that prehuman past, but only a faint proof, and *there* was the neat link he shared with the bird: It was a faint ghost of the once gargantuan, sublime stature of its reigning ancestors, just as every movement, every breath and blinking of an eye, were all a faint ghost of the once bright-burning, feverish passion that reigned in Rigo's life.

The goose hopped down onto the old, brittle linoleum floor. It shook its wings some more, unfamiliar with the cooler temperature of the indoors, the nauseating stench of indescribable chemicals, and on top of all, the stench of *humans*. It dared not even take a single, cautious step just then. It would shake its wings, widening itself to stand as a mighty foe in the process, and with its glassy, aquamarine eyes, it would watch for a while.

Rigo didn't think to alert the nurses. Perhaps it was because even then he may have felt the tug of something wondrous and terrible about to happen, and so he chose to let it run uninterrupted. Equally likely, however, was the simple fact that Rigo could not be bothered to do much of anything anymore. These final days he always felt like asking for help was like a man whose stomach has been torn to shreds begging the starved for some food. His sheets were only changed when the nurses noticed the staleness in the room and the sulfurous, rotten smell about his bed, but even then, they were so hurriedly changed that those same nurses still failed to notice the cobwebs knit at every corner, the broken-off bits of wall and floor, and the shut-off machinery from tests performed weeks previous that needed to be wheeled out, their many interconnecting cables in complete disorder like spilled guts surrendered in utter failure.

The goose quickly got bold and pecked at the cables, but, realizing it was nothing tasty, it decided to finally make a move forward. In a short journey of three steps, it got its feet tangled in one of the cables and almost tripped, making a spattering of sounds across the floor and a ruffling of wings that sounded like cloth being shaken. It stood perfectly still right after, for the first time becoming aware of another presence in that room (the presence reeking strongest of that overpowering, fleshy smell). It could now only see this other being as a set of dry feet dangling from the edge of the bed. Wasting no time and finding more courage in this possible encounter, it took another few steps forward.

Rigo lost sight of the creature after it hopped down from the window. He figured it could not have gotten far and was probably still at the foot of the bed. For some reason, it made him happy to be a participant in this private encounter, amused at where it might lead, if only just a few bed sheets covered in bird shit. He knew it would be days until someone, understandably bewildered, would change the terminally ill maricón's bedsheets and find the goose droppings on it, then eye one or two discarded feathers left behind by the intruder as the only other token of its visit. Rigo laughed thinking they might even go to the nearby library and research whether this fearsome, unknown disease also turned the patient into a fucking chicken. Then he sighed thinking how it *would* indeed be days until someone checked in. The entire facility hardly had any staff or resources to keep track of every sick and dying soul that haunted its beds, so their time was better spent elsewhere rather than near the doomed. It was an abandoned room that housed him, the fuses that still directed electricity into it waiting only for his last, rancid breath before shutting off completely. That is all that had been left to his name: A hospital room that would soon be shut down, and a small placard with his and Nacho's names. When the councilmember had, weeks before, gone into that room to inform him of this heroic feat—placing special emphasis on how Rigo and Nacho would go down in history as the couple that fought, that demanded awareness, demanded action, demanded respect for "their kind," in a nation sadly mired in prejudice and hate, etc.—Rigo had nearly flown at his throat with his bare teeth in unbridled, white-hot anger. Swallowing that empty rage, however, he had only shaken the politician's soft, weak hand and tried his hardest to smile at him but in the end could not bring himself to do so. All else be damned, it had been Nacho's dream to leave a mark just like that—a monument for "the cause"—and so Rigo would let him have his selfish wish. In any other eyes, Rigo would have been the selfish one—the envious boyfriend trying to drag his man down from the spotlight as a leading activist for "their kind" and into the greedy, dark clutches of their bedroom—but what did any of them know? Sure, they would get their memorial, their placard with the couple's names on it to parade for political benefit, for halfhearted gestures towards a "progressive future," for the memory of who they saw Nacho as. However, Rigo had been pleased when the prototype placard had been unveiled before his body, the displayer getting it as close to Rigo as he dared, lest he be infected with whatever was wasting this miserable soul away. Thankfully, it was close enough so that Rigo could read both names: Ignacio Puentes and Rigoberto Villalobos. Rigo gave the approval they needed, was brought up to a sitting position by a silent nurse so that he could sign some documents (and how alien the pen had felt in his hand, like an icy kiss from an old life—from its trivial, everyday matters like writing, signing papers, taking a test at school—all of which would soon cease to have meaning within those walls that eagerly awaited only his death), and then, when they had all finally gone and left him alone to resume his quiet waiting, he stretched the bed back down as far as it went and finally smiled as he dozed off into his third nap that day. They could have their placard and their room, and Nacho could have his selfish wish, but it would be under *his* conditions. Thus, Rigo let the room wear away to an aspect befitting its one and final guest, allowing the rancidness to reign at any corner it chose to settle in. As for the placard people, they would get their Ignacio and their Rigoberto, but they would *never* get *Rigo* and his *Nacho*. They would never get those private names, whispered in each other's ears in between nibbled earlobes, in the midst of dark, fevered exchanges of embraces, kisses, and fluids—fluids as light as the moisture between lips, and as heavy, as mortal, as intimately monstrous as those that had birthed the voracious disease that had taken Nacho forever and was now wearing away at the sole bearer of his memory with such impassioned barbarity. No, they would not get Nacho. Not *his* Nacho. *Never* his Nacho. They could have all the information that would maybe even make it into school textbooks, all the important details about Ignacio Puentes, a man who fought for "his kind," but what use was any of that to truly cement his remembrance? What candle could dates and important events in history hold to knowing that ridges of his back or the number of moles along his shoulders? They would never be able to describe the shade of those dark spots, darker than even his already tanned skin, like rich earth covering Rigo every night, pulling inward and burying him with every stroke as he felt every one of Nacho's heartbeats against his own chest. That was a noise that no one else would ever hear or describe, a beat that would never again resume, and was there only as a distant tune that still had an air of the sweet and tender, even in Rigo's decimated state. All knowledge of where his skin paled into a creamy beige, of what his voice moaned when it was just them pouring into each other, all of that would die with Rigo, and the greedy, self-interested world would never get it—

The goose heard a surprised yelp when its beak nipped at one of the toes above. The foot recoiled with surprising strength, knocking its beak aside. The bird retained composure, unusually calm even after such a rude assault. Somehow, the contact of skins had smoothed its beastly brain down to a softer demeanor. The bird, too, felt that there was something about to tie them together.

Rigo felt almost indignant, having been bitten by his visitor even after making zero fuss about its intrusion. Still, the hot pain the damned thing's beak had left on his big toe felt strangely good. Then he thought he had truly lost it, laughing at his own pathetic nonlife spent inside that room, and how that bite was the only real, unrestrained contact with another living thing he had had in months. The hands that rarely washed him and changed sheets and moved the bundle of needles along his wrists felt colder, like machines built only to help the process along, a long conveyor belt directing him into the mouth of that lonely, static thing called death. The spontaneity of this new apparition and the unpredictability of its intentions made Rigo feel a nostalgic warmth inside. He had felt the same enveloping warmth—a lot like a flushing of the face from concern or even fear, but ultimately reassurance that everything would be fine in the end—whenever he was in the clutches of one of Nacho's plans. The same, familiar glow now ebbing from the tip of his toe to the center point of his mind's eye was the same he had felt when Nacho first crossed his sight outside the lecture hall on his first year, on his first-ever college class, just as he had almost decided to turn around and find a bus stop to take him back home, back to the disappointed faces of his parents who had proudly paraded how he was the only one in his family to ever get this far, to ever set foot off their town to chase a dream that big. He had felt that piercing hotness at once in those calm, reassuring eyes staring directly at him, *just* at him, that entire, glowing-hot gaze just for him, and telling him, *Stay*. Then, at every instance of close proximity, of elevated stakes, elevated emotion as he tackled problem after problem in the unshakable hardness of Nacho's embrace, the warmth was there. It was there when Rigo first heard his voice, both in the casualness of their first handshake, then in the ensnaring coils of their passion the first time they made love—not *fucked*, but made love, after an opening number of quick, clumsy, and thoughtless encounters made them aware that they were, indeed, addicted to each other's caresses, each other's whispered words of love and adoration. The warmth was there when Nacho took him to his first protest, Rigo aware that he was only there for Nacho, spellbound by the passion of his statements over the loudspeaker, mesmerized by his leadership, his courage—all of these being the only qualities from his political toil that had helped set ablaze their passion even further. The warmth was there when they first moved in together. The warmth was there when Nacho helped him tell his parents about them. It was there when they embraced, drunk on mezcal, in the boiling hot motel room near his hometown after they'd been run out by his parents, the last time Rigo had been anywhere near his old home. With the words "putos" and "jotos" dancing drunkenly and distant in his brain as the mezcal softened and boiled everything, he had instead found a new home in those ceaseless embraces, those kisses and lickings and thrusts that reassured him *this* was a home that would not budge even in the strongest storm. The warmth was there when Nacho was open about why he would never fuck him raw, why so much caution around it, why they couldn't truly touch in the barest sense that Rigo yearned for. It was there as it became Rigo's turn to comfort, through tears that seemed like they would never stop that night, and embrace *his* Nacho, Rigo for the first time holding on to these hopes he had often heard from "the movement," the distant whispers of a cure soon, of a pill or treatment to promote longevity, anything to help him resettle into those dreams he vainly clutched, dreams of their happiness being an eternal and uncompromised thing, the word "death" still not carrying the totality it was emblazoned with when Nacho died in his sleep—that goddamned, deceitful sleep that never let him say goodbye. The warmth was there as they had waited for results after the condom tore, something that had felt so small and brief like moving a finger, but which swiftly bled into their binds with the tantalizing force of its danger. As they were told they were now both positive, Rigo felt incredible anger, not at Nacho, but at the cruelly mundane thing that had sealed both their fates, thinking to how their ancestors must have met their deaths with heavy cuts from obsidian knives, in the tugs of some fierce battle, in the honor of their erected city housing their glory, and here *they* were, two bodies, skins just as bronze, who loved just as (if not more) passionately and burningly as those warriors, those poets, those deities of times past, and they were to die over "se reventó el condón," a phrase so clinical, so pragmatic and distant from what their lovemaking had truly meant, had truly been driven by. In the mutual wait for their demise the warmth had grown duller, more painful to ingest at times, but still there, keeping them attached to each other's thinning, wilting limbs, keeping them tied to their kisses that grew tremblier with each day, and it grew just a bit stronger when, even after their copulation had betrayed them, it brought them together again, their bodies still understanding just how to move in each other's rhythms, explore each other's pleasure with patience and hungry, emaciated love, their diseased fucking making the hospital just a bit less ugly, and making their bed, with its remote controls and thin, uncomfortable mattress, feel like a lovers' bed again. The warmth had been there when Nacho had joked as he held Rigo's hand, joked about someone having burned his Dorian Gray picture, making his sins and shame truly show in this newly ugly body of his. Rigo did not want to laugh at this, but he had done so only because Nacho had laughed first. Just after that, Nacho had sat Rigo down to tell him who had given him the disease, which they had never talked about before. Only out of respect, he listened to Nacho describe this mysterious lover who Rigo could not resent or hate or feel jealousy for in the end, for he understood then what it meant to die over a disease shared in intimacy, to die by poison administered through kisses and caresses. The warmth had last been there when Nacho had drunk from a cup in Rigo's hand the day before he died. Nacho had barely taken a few gulps when he smacked his lips, winked at Rigo, and said, "Gracias, guapo. ¿Eres soltero?" And now, the warmth, just as sumptuous, just as melancholy and all-consuming, was there again in that goose bite, the source of it surely perched somewhere inside the creature's beak.

The goose made the final decision to climb the bed. It once more beat its wings clumsily, so unaccustomed to flight, but driven by this newfound need to meet its companion face-to-face. In a rush of flutters and more discarded feathers that fell in slow-motion and refracted sunlight in beams like white embers, the goose's feet scratched at the foot of the bed, gaining a tenuous balance as its wings continued to labor for control of the airs. The stench of humans seemed highest at the top of this mount. Without fear, the goose gained momentum and ascended just enough so that its webbed, rugged feet landed firmly on the bedsheets bundled around a thin, dark figure.

Rigo had never believed in anything spiritual like reincarnation or messages from beyond. Surely, it would have been the superstitious answer someone from his family would have given to this weird meeting taking place (and in wondering so, he felt the dull sting of remembering how there was no knowing if anyone from his family would dare visit and see him in his final days, something he both dreaded and awaited with torturous patience). At first, he had only begun feeling some discomfort and worry over the significantly sized bird hopping onto his bed. Having watched it previously only from the distance of the window, he had only noted a white blob in the rough shape of a goose running across the drying grass of the hospital yard, performing its relentless, almost ritualistic attacks on anyone nearby, then simply standing around, wings still proudly raised, waiting for its next chance to charge. It had been amusing watching it nip at ladies holding sandwiches, at kids getting close to it on a dare, and especially at poor nurses just trying to innocently walk back to their cars. Now, however, being fully aware of its short temper and considerable size and strength, Rigo viewed the thing as a possible threat. There indeed was something primitive about its features, something that seemed incongruous with the manmade building that now held it, something in the vein of "running from a predator deep in the jungle" about its rugged, sharp talons, something cold and inscrutable in its piercing eyes that held instincts older than man, in its beak shaped like a flattened dagger. Rigo was sure he'd still have the strength to push it away if it tried anything with him, but he had no way of knowing how persistent the bird could be, and long and arduous strain was not in Rigo's favor. Still, the warmth that ran around his nipped toe, up his legs which he had thought long since dead, was tempting enough that he allowed the beast to remain in bed with him.

The goose squirted shit on the sheets, droppings the gray color of cement that ran down off the edge of the bed, lightly perfumed of grass. It adopted a weird stance, stretching its wings as far as they went, as if readying either an attack or an embrace. Its beak pointed upwards at the ceiling, beckoning to the flickering fluorescent light as it would to the sun. Then, without a drawing of breath, without warning, it let out three honking screeches as loud as human screams, resounding in the empty halls of that hospital wing.

Rigo sat up in awe. The display was mesmerizing. He detected zero aggression from the animal. Somehow, he knew the display was one of invitation, the bird showing itself exposed and vulnerable like that, letting out its guttural cries like begging for attention. He had to stop himself from reaching out and touching it, knowing such a swift movement might be trying the bird's trustworthiness. Still, his eyes, so used to their grimacing position, lit up with a brightness that had once only been possible when a part of him was in the teeth of his dead lover, nibbling around his hands, about his chest, tantalizingly close to clamping down on a nipple or a bit on his thigh, or simply kissing him, leaving cool trails of drool all over his skin. Here was that light again, in the form of a tall and fearsome beast bearing its heart out to him. Where tears had once been thought forever halted, not even spilling for the burial of his lost half, they now ran freely, perhaps due to the sheer absurdity this vision provoked, which nonetheless felt heavenly fated, even if in a caricature way.

The goose ceased its rigid pose and resumed the pace of its journey, never taking its eyes off its target. It walked in a straight line across the abdomen, which barely felt like anything, wasted and flattened as it was. Along the goose's long neck, the bristling sensation extended up and down, a sensation that danced around its serrated tongue, at the edges of its hardened beak like ants crawling at hypnotic pace, something that told it to proceed. Somewhere along the human's chest, it stopped dead in its tracks, and in a diving motion, its neck bent forward to catch a deeper glimpse into the human's eyes. Just then, a gust of wind blew in through the window, blowing the curtains about as the sun neared its own meeting with the horizon, making the bright orange rays dance through the fluttering curtains, lighting the room in fragmented gold that bounced within the dimness of all else.

Rigo saw the bird bathed in gold just as it sat on his chest. In its almost blinding glory, he felt its searing touch and visage completely eclipse all other thoughts in his head. In that room, in that honey-colored beauty of dying daylight, in that queer coupling now unfolding, it was only him and this animal, this glowing, mighty beast. Just then, Rigo wondered if all those days of exchanging glances with the bird had been by the animal's own design as well. He wondered (the part of him telling him this was all madness growing invisible) if all those days that it had chased its victims around, if all of that had also been a display, a private dance just for Rigo's eyes. He wondered for how long the bird had been planning this encounter, if it was its first time learning of the window being wide open, or if it had made previous, unperceived visits, perhaps perching at the windowsill late into the night while Rigo slept through his always restless sleep. He wondered if the bird had thought of entering but could never bring itself to have the courage of going that extra nudge, that extra pull towards that figure it had chosen as its destined partner, the fulfillment of that longingness they had cast at each other from a distance, even if unaware. Now Rigo could barely resist the beast, burying his fingers in its divinely hot feathers. Before he knew it, his hand had slipped under its left wing, feeling burning hot from the simple contact. It was the way he felt the aliveness of it writhe under his finger, felt the taciturn thumping of the wondrous tools that design sentience, that made him realize he had not felt that living beating of another being in what seemed centuries. In his tearful face dawned momentarily the memory, again, of the passionate lovemaking Nacho had made to him towards the end of his life, as if in a last-ditch attempt of at least retaining dignity.

Keeping his disease from taking that as well, he had thrust deep inside him, feeling engorged, bathed in newfound vigor, showing the disease that its acid, which had condemned them, could not eat away at itself, nor at their love, and so, both diseased, they became like acid themselves, burning not in flames but in their sizzling erosion, aggressively convulsing atop each other until they were completely exhausted, having fed each other death again with their sex. When the bird bent its neck and fixed its electric blue eyes right into his own, he felt the same pleasurable corrosion run along his spine, the same longing to melt away into his union with Nacho, into the act that had both sealed their fate and still stood as the biggest expression of the desperate craving they had for each other. Rigo felt a plea escape his lips just as he felt the jolt from his libido thunder across his body when their human and animal gazes locked, realizing for the first time that he was fully erect under the bird's weight. He didn't manage to attach words to this sound he let out, but its painful supplication was unignorable: A further taste of that warmth that was like live coals in his hands, both of them now buried under the beast's wings like in a loving embrace.

The goose dove its beak straight into the man's chest, tasting the first drops of blood drawn from the paper-thin skin. It then set to work at pecking in and out of the opening wound, maneuvering its beak with dexterity as it dug deeper and deeper. The human made no sound, no gesture, no effort to swipe him away. What at first was just a redness from its nips soon became a hole with freshly unearthed sinews screaming in bright pinks and reds along the exposed area around the light blue hospital gown. The goose labored with surprising strength, with a vigor it had never spent on meat laid out so easily before it yet drawn to its destruction like nothing else had ever drawn its cold blood and restless eyes. The blood now covered its orange beak, coating it in a dark, almost maroon gloss that dripped all the way to its white feathers, like hot, hot blood coating the cool and calm face of a mound of snow.

Rigo was speechless. The first few nips had been much like the one at his toe: warm, playful, strangely pleasant, so that he had not noticed when the redness turned into blood coating his chest. Looking up now he saw the beast hard at work uncoiling all his inner arrangements, unbothered by the bleeding now smeared across its entire face and dripping down its long neck. Of all things felt, Rigo felt the pain the least, only a constant tugging and the heaviness of each bite pressing down near his solar plexus, like something infinite and colossal settling on him ounce by ounce. What he felt the most, as he had suspected when the bird first presented itself encased in the amber glow of the late afternoon, was the hotness that was now like melted glass flowing into his dirty veins. He tried closing his eyes, perhaps in a last, desperate attempt at retreating into himself and his pain to fully assess the reality of the situation: That a creature had broken into his room and was now fatally injuring him. However, his eyes remained open, basking in the glory of the beast hard at work searching for the one string of flesh that would forever unstitch him from that bed, that room, those soiled, failing moments that were his last days of life. The bird made small sounds like nervous, wet chewing, and its droppings, along with the open window with curtains still flowing, brought in an earthy smell of outdoors that Rigo had not experienced so up-close in so long. Since having been bedbound, sealed into the old, closed-up smell of his deathbed, he had not experienced such openness, the liberated wildness of nature, as he was now, impaled in the beak of this creature. With fingers twitching as if begging the rest of him to do something, he watched, noting the bird's body bobbing softly up and down as it dug deeper, inch by inch, decided to undo him in soft, almost loving strokes and kisses. How it reminded him of Nacho just then, laid atop him, working himself in and out and in and out of him, with each thrust trying to break him apart. He had never asked Nacho if he felt guilty of having been the one to seal Rigo's fate along with his. Rigo never knew what Nacho's relationship was to this disease on those last days, only that he kept his rigid stance during his speeches, spoke with the same convictions, the same passionate search for social justice, while within their bedsheets, he felt the complete aggression and passion he spared from the public's eye. Now, nakedly locked in a similarly brutal passion with this bird, Rigo had to admit to himself that he *had* felt, on some occasions, as if Nacho had really killed him, as if his cock were not an instrument for impassioned fucking but a sharp blade made to gut and ruin, and he had enjoyed the feeling immensely, given himself up as the one thing Nacho would drag to his grave with him. With that same fatal desire to claim and undo, Rigo saw the bird dig its beak further and further into the mangled, distorted hole in his chest that was now as big as his fist.

The goose dug until it chanced upon something moving and steaming. The thing beat slower and slower, and from it, a great gush of blood spurted outwards when the beak hit it. It was more of that near-tasteless water that now nearly covered its entire upper half, water heavy with something that made it sulfuric, somewhat bitter in the goose's barely discerning tongue. With more eagerness, it dug its tongue into the spasming, tougher meat. From that hole it drank, tore bits off, fed just as a songbird bathes and refreshes at a water fountain.

Rigo recalled reading of Greek gods descending as swan, of disembodied voices from those already claimed by death returning as the songs of birds, the watchful eyes of pitch-black ravens perched atop busts and articulating the last, pained words of hurt and restless lovers. Yet, as all of this crossed his mind, he ultimately settled on the last thought of his failing fingers plucking out a feather from under the bird's wing. Nacho's image fell from his eyes, and instead, peeled and dried from not blinking, he stared at this bird, this intrusion, this unexpected twist that now had his half-eaten heart clenched tightly in its beak. He moved to pluck more feathers, but his hands fell to his sides, defeated. He heard no footsteps, no panic, and he knew he was completely alone in his death. He wanted to speak something to the bird, the only one that would hear him, but just then, it once more raised its head and honked to the ceiling, a sound like open pastures, vast hills that housed the very nature this beast had dragged in through the window to be Rigo's last companion in his moment of death. With the same bitter passion that had clung him to Nacho when he found his dead body, when he would not wake after all the vicious shaking and screaming from Rigo and his dry, tearless cries that sounded more like a feigned tantrum begging him to return, with the same passion when he felt Nacho's skin hardened like rock, his eyes closed tightly, the doctors never allowing Rigo one final look at those brown, intense eyes that knew him with deeper intimacy than nothing else—with all that same passion, Rigo begged the bird, "Come closer. Please, come closer," in a voice as ragged as his half-eaten heart.

The goose, drenched in blood, still tasting the rugged flesh this human hid beneath, ceased its honking and looked back down, hearing something pass through the human's lips, a sound just like breathing, just as low and meaningless.

Rigo wanted to reach out again but couldn't. He felt too weak, still feeling new, hot blood spurting out from his chest. His breathing grew rushed, his eyes glazed over as the light from the window lowered more, giving way to the dark nothingness of nighttime. Then he felt his mouth creep upwards into a smile.

The goose walked further up along the man's body until its posterior was directly sat atop the newly opened wound from which it had fed.

Rigo was smiling because the hidden pains of his disease were finally lifting. After so long, they had grown almost unnoticeable, yet their departure was profusely felt. *Nothing* hurt. Nothing weighed on him just then except this bird that now positioned itself right above his flayed chest, warming it the way a mother warms a cut or bruise with a tiny kiss. He felt something long and wormy crawl into his wounds, dressing them with a viscous balm that cooled that burnt pit left in him. He felt like all about his body now there were those downy, soft feathers, nuzzling him almost in apology. His eyes and strength were finally dwindling back to being nothing, to join the place one could only enter as dust, where his lover now reveled in that mercy of knowing nothing of the world of the living.

As the goose positioned its rear atop the wound, its long, barbed, twisted penis inserted itself into the exposed skin, right down into the crude hole its beak had carved into the human's heart. Without thrusts, without any expended strength, the penis splurged forth a small load of semen, barely squeezing forth in cold, unseen drops that soon got lost inside the unseen depths of this new recipient.

Rigo felt the gift, felt it come inside him as easily and smoothly as any other time Nacho may have wanted to claim him as his for the night. Then, the last few thumps of his heart felt incredibly loud, announcing the last time the organ would carry out its duty. He wondered if Nacho had felt the same, or if, because of sleep, he had felt nothing at all, had not even felt the grief of leaving Rigo lost and abandoned behind. Rigo was then grateful to be fully awake, fully conscious of the indescribable sensation now overtaking him. Then, it became too tiring to think about Nacho. It became too tiring to think of anything other than this creature from unknown parts now delicately prostrated above the fatal wound. With what ease, with what natural form and purpose it had entered through that window. With what ease it had carved itself an adequate hole for its kind of lovemaking. With what ease it now remained atop him, looking down, boldly, without regret, even without reason, maybe completely unaware of what it had just done to him. Rigo tried reaching out one last time and could not. He wondered if maybe the bird would eat the rest of him, but he had not felt hunger in those bites. It was playfulness and... dare he say it, *lust*, that had guided the fowl's attack. Rigo recognized this in the creature as both their eyes half-closed in satisfied ecstasy. Both tired from their labor, Rigo decided it was enough. He was happy to have shared himself with another living being without harm, without regret, without more tragedy sprouting forth from his disease. He was happy to have become sustenance, to have become a bitemark, a hole that this brute animal could make its own, and that they had been joined by this mutual tug of war where the bird had been triumphant in turning off Rigo's pain, his synapses, his longing, and the hidden, stunted lust that made his member retain its angry hardness even after his heart had stopped beating. In one last look, forever fixed on the bird, Rigo saw it spread its wings once more, in that pose that it so loved, and then stand on its webbed feet again, screech again, and while it retained that stance, Rigo died in the midst of the sybaritic fear that had gripped him since the beast had entered.

The goose noticed the human wasn't moving anymore. Once more, it pecked at the wound, but even these tugs managed to rouse nothing. Its penis receded and its webbed feet scratched lightly at the exposed skin of the man. Once more, it let out its cries, its wings flapping furiously, as if wanting to achieve flight, but also wanting to stay planted atop this figure. As if possessed by more of those unknown winds that had led it there, it zoomed around the room, knocking over equipment, the IV drip still attached to the man's arm, the hoses flying like gutted veins with drips of blood splashed across the dirty white linen of the bed. The goose was unrelenting, breaking expensive machines, tearing at the curtains that now only let the dark of night waft in imposing, all-consuming. It left its droppings and feathers scattered everywhere, along with scratches and vicious bites on the wires and the paint chipping off the walls. All about was the evidence of its entrance, and its unwillingness to ever leave, its desire to leave its mark seeping deeply into that room.

The goose's destruction had alerted hurried feet that scrambled to the second floor, astonished that the ever-quiet corner of that building was in such commotion. The panicking nurses found the toppled heart monitor beeping its single note loudly, the spilled medicines and serums that now mixed with bird shit and feathers on the floor, and the soiled bed big enough to carry two wasted lovers. The first to arrive also found the goose in its glorious pose, with the grace of its long neck curved gently around the head of its victim with wings stretched outward, defying anyone who might want to disturb their rest, softly cooing at Rigo, immobile, while its feathers bristled and one of its feet touched his hardened hand, fitting snugly inside his inert grip. One lone, bitter tear bled from a piercing blue eye and down into the sheets that covered its newfound roost.

GROWING LOVE

I felt his tiny murmurs falling somewhere at my liver. They hit like warm little blood-soaked kisses, tickling whispers babbling nonsense, but then his words, even without sound or meaning, took shape, took a pulse, and felt like a hand, touching things that were never to be touched. They squeezed at my entrails with impossible intimacy, and I understood.

And I loved it.

I held my side while lying in bed, trying to cradle whatever segment of flesh he currently nestled in, whatever piece of fat or tissue he took as his bed. I could not feel him, per se, but I felt a resounding *him* all over, like loud bass noise reverberating up and down my entire frame, echoing with a pleasure that made me curl my toes, wanting nothing but to lie there and feel it forever. Along my esophagus, I felt air rise like a burp, but not a burp. It was lovelier, lighter than gas, lighter than air, and when it cracked through my throat, with a taste like citrus and sugar, I felt it finally take the shape of a word through my teeth: "Love."

He loved sending these messages to reassure me, like miniature smoke signals lovingly burned somewhere in the pit of my stomach. I closed my eyes, heavy with pleasure, and I slept cradled in the constant pulsing of his care.

I dreamed, but my dream was simply of lying there, as if being there was already the culmination of every bit of joy my mind could imagine. I only knew it was a dream because I could not move, and instead of having to feel for him somewhere in my gut, he emerged. I felt him dance out through my tongue in honeyed steps, and when I finally laid eyes on him I was aghast at his smallness, how so much love and beauty could fit into such a minuscule frame, about the size of a finger. Yet, it was easy to see how this small, small thing stunned and enveloped me so, with its gossamer skin shining with its own natural glow, soft and immaculate, like a single drop of flesh that had fallen from heaven itself, some stray piece of firmament accidentally discarded while another angel was being fashioned from celestial ichor and flame. Surely, it had plummeted with graceful and almost obscene beauty all the way from up there, too pure for this world, crashing through the atmosphere until by some wild chance it landed here, with me, for me to own and house in my innermost parts. I watched him dance along the firm flatness of my chest, skip about in the crook near my armpit, and rest his feet sitting atop the mound of my left nipple.

For how long would he dance and frolic?

Forever, I hoped.

"David," I heard him, not so much saying it as *provoking* it in the eye of my mind.

Such was his language: warm waves washing over me, a change in the air that twisted in just the right way to have me understand. I did not need hearing to grasp his speech. His presence and influence were enough, but it was only in dreams that I understood. I often wondered if the dreams were also his own crafting. I wondered if he had somehow managed to cast his charms even in the darkest corners of the brain where dreams are made. I also wondered, however, if they were just my own desire, if maybe I was just madly lost in adoration, and the dreams were a natural proceeding. All I can say is that, within our symbiosis, these details did not matter. We shared a world of dreams as lovers share a bed.

"David," he provoked again. "I will eat now. I will eat now. I'm so hungry."

These last statements had a coarseness to them, whereas my name always felt sweet and lulling. Whenever he let me know of his hunger, it always felt like rough, hardened fingers against my temples. For the third time since our first meeting (a meeting I could not recall—it seemed our wondrous marriage was a thing blurred and worn by eons) he wanted to eat, and his urge felt bigger and wilder than before. The space between each feeding had gotten shorter, too. Maybe there was a call for alarm then, yet what I feared most in that instance was that he was leaving. He had to leave me to feed, and that thought horrified me.

"No!" I said out loud, as if someone had just offered to amputate a limb. My voice, my clumsy need for oral noise, sounded so ugly against the ethereal prickling of such beautiful and subliminal a language as his. Still, I felt a maddened urge to scream and stop him. "Stay in me!" I yelled. "Stay in me!"

Then I felt that devastating pain I had felt twice before now, on each of his outings, like my very heart torn from my chest, hot and steaming with the vital blood it would no longer feed me, leaving behind only a cold and mangled hole. Each of my veins was now haunted by an excruciating loneliness. My stomach caved in, deflated down to a wrinkle, robbed of its comfortable fullness. All of me felt dead, and I knew that this was the coldness of a death very much real. Yet, it clashed with the awareness of a mind very much alive, and the effect was unbearable, as if I was expected to see my flesh rot, to feel my organs fail, and to double over against the insurmountable ache that folds any mortal soul, but without the mercy of unconsciousness.

I swung over to my side, managing to wake myself up. I was sore all over, like one big gash had been opened straight down the middle of my whole being, as if I was just limbs attached to one dry, hollow socket. It wasn't until minutes into wakefulness that I realized I was moaning, salty tears and mucus already smeared across my face. It was the countenance of someone who had already sunk years into a withered love that would never revive.

I *had* to find where he had gone off to.

I stumbled off my bed and searched for him with blind hands across the floor, hoping he wasn't too far away. Shivering, I thought to feel my skin. It was icy and dry. I felt riddled with an ugliness that sunk all the way *in*. The sharp pain all along my back confirmed that he had indeed taken off. And I *needed* him. From all fours, I tried to gain some footing and managed to rise onto my knees, where I had a better view of my room. Ripped school papers and the contents of gutted drawers were strewn about, and finally my eyes fell on the open door of my bedroom.

I managed to stand, and, shaking off dizziness, I noticed there had been a stench lingering around my nostrils, and I somehow recognized it for what it was: blood and shit. I looked over to my bed and my hand shot up to cover my mouth, holding in a loud gasp. My sheets were drenched in the stuff, a big dark spot against the white bedding. It was black in color under the little moonlight that crept in through the window shutters. Now along with my mortal fear of having lost him came a new creeping fear, almost making me forget my previous worries: A fear that he had seriously wounded me, that I would bleed out and fall dead on my own filth. I felt around the seat of my pajama pants and felt them seeped in moisture, a frayed hole ripped at the center. I held back tears and stumbled out of my room.

I thought I saw him languidly pacing at the corner of the hallway, but it was only my cat Jinx entertained by some stray sliver of starlight that fell on the carpet from the hallway window. I was gasping with desperation now, and on the seemingly endless tumble down the stairs, I almost fainted. Still, I was happy to have seen dad's bedroom door was still securely shut.

Thoughts groggily danced around my head as wakefulness came in with bigger gulps of air. There had never been blood before. He had never forced his way out before. Even his previous exits had been in the mildly uncomfortable strain of a bowel movement, not this aggressive ripping and tearing. As if some narcotic's effects were finally lifting, an unperceived fogginess in my eyes waning, I realized what I had been doing, what had been living inside me, and that I was desperate to let it back in. My steps hesitated more as I reached the threshold of the kitchen, unsure if I really wanted to have this meeting anymore. Still, the coldness and emptiness prevailed, along with a thirst which I knew would never be quenched unless I found him.

The kitchen was surprisingly intact. His previous feedings had consisted of scraps of raw meat and some milk he had managed to dig out from the fridge, and it had been enough for him to return to me, silent and content. Here, once more, my fear escalated as a wild array of thoughts now dawned on me: *What could he have chosen to feed on this time? What else did he crave from this home? Would he return? Would he? Would he?*

My energy was slowly returning, and so was my composure as I realized, although bloody, his exit hadn't made any fatal wounds. I didn't feel any more wetness. The blood around my pants was drying, and no new blood leaked out. Still, the emptiness of my stomach begged for him. I *needed* him. I really did. Even after all the horror, the disgust and uncertainty, even knowing the unsavory reality of our coupling, I could not help it. My center was piercing frost. I felt at any moment I would slip into death, the fatal pangs of this privation growing deeper, heavier.

I heard a sucking sound coming from the living room. There, in the corner adorned with potted plants, I found him. I had seen him twice before, but the true image of his physicality always evaded me whenever he returned, always washed away by the constant, gentle pushing of that ecstasy he made me dream of. Here, however, in the stark cold of the outside, as I carried the putrid emptiness he left behind, I nearly stumbled back out of sheer terror at this vision. What I saw was not the heavenly blessing that danced along my chest in dreams. It stood on all eight limbs, bathed in darkness, only a tar-black blob making those horrid sucking sounds, wet and vicious. I took some steps back towards the light switch by the front door. It was the sliding kind, and I pulled it up just enough to illuminate the scene but dim enough to protect myself from really taking in the horrid details of the thing. I crept back towards it and stood behind the couch, both fascinated and repulsed, and saw it with more clarity.

Along its tadpole-shaped body was the spiderweb pattern of white blisters. The skin from which those blisters grew was dull and gray like rotten cooked meat. The eight fat stumps that jutted out from its underside ended in single bone-white claws which now scraped greedily against the wooden floor, an apparent gesture of pleasure as its maw, which revealed some needle-like teeth that hung over its black lips, clicked with the sound of falling toothpicks as it continued sucking on whatever it was feeding on. It had no eyes. It did not need them, I figured, when it made my dark and soft insides its home. That thought made me bend down with a full-body shiver. I instantly felt what I had been too drunk with delight to fully grasp: That this thing had lived in me, rubbed those very same blisters along my stomach lining, sweated that viscous discharge into the food I ate, and who knew what other unspeakable things it entertained itself doing when it had plenty of time to make itself comfortable in the cover of my flesh and blood. I also noticed it was larger this time, as previously ignored memories crawled back. Whereas before it had been the size of a finger, now, after having seemingly found something more substantial to eat, it had grown to about the size of my fist.

As I looked up slowly, trying not to startle it, for I figured it still had not perceived me, I finally noticed the plants it stood between. The once vibrant parlor palms were now withered down to yellow-brown, desiccated twigs and leaves. No life was left in any of them, as if something had managed to tap into the very vein that life flows through and drain it down to the last drop. Now the culprit relished the last few drops of the lifeforce it had somehow managed to crack open and feast on. I did not know where it had conceived of this weird diet, but the raw meat and milk had not been enough. Those, it seemed, had only carried an afterthought of life, the faintest hint of a perfume that it had found much more potent in the actual living things that it got its thirsty lips on.

I sobbed loudly. It stopped its hideous lip-smacking at the sound of my voice, finally noticing me, but I could not contain myself. My dead mother's plants were gone. I lit up with unprecedented rage, clenching my fists, as if just now for the first time in my life having felt the full grief of my mother's passing. Decided on finding something with which to crush the wretched thing, I no longer cared about the unseemly void its absence left. However, still trapped in that weak and sorry state it left me in, I was slow to react and failed to notice it no longer fed in the corner of the living room. By the time I thought to move and search for it again, it was scurrying up my leg with alarming swiftness. I figured it did not want to have me realize too many things as the cuffs of its spell slowly wore out. It was desperate to come back and bathe me in dreams again. I tried in vain to catch it between my fingers, but it was already scratching at my teeth and cutting at my gums with its many claws, trying to find its way inside again. My fingers slipped through its viscosity. It was impossible to grab it. The most I managed to do was to burst a few of its blisters, but that only made it harder to clutch as it oozed more grease. It didn't appear to be in any pain. It only cared about returning.

Finally it managed to nudge three of its claws somewhere around my jaw hinges, as if it knew all too well the mechanisms that opened the doors of my body. With ease, it flung my mouth open, its tooth-lined stoma scurrying in first and scraping all along my tongue like a long and bitter kiss. I did not think I would be able to pass the burgeoning mass it had now become. Instantly the leftover grime of blood and shit still coating its body flared into a noxious, stinging taste of bile that clung to my tongue and nose, making the air feel thin and sharp. Hot vomit rose up along my throat, but it must have burrowed right past it and shoved it back down. I no longer tried to grasp its body, knowing it was useless. I fell to my knees, eyes burning and watering, my air passage shut as the thing danced further down, its blistery body rubbing my inner cheeks as it burrowed in spins like a drill. Along my teeth more blisters burst, the grease and pus swishing with drool. I begged for my taste to somehow give out, but my tongue was painfully alive with sensation. I keeled over and hoped it would finish passing through faster.

And then it felt good again. Then I felt it resettled in the nook where it belonged, like a missing limb reattaching and the stitchwork feeling like a delicate massage that cooled wounds that nothing else could touch. Even with its bigger size, it only felt like the pleasure it brought was twofold now, and then, as the waves of calm billowed up my spine, it wasn't *it* but *him* again, whispering with subtle touches his apologies and his lovingness. "Love" is what I felt all over.

"Love."

"Love."
"Love."

I forgot all about the previous incident and managed to crawl to the living room couch, where I lay down and basked in the warmth as if the sun had never set that night. I cradled my abdomen in both arms like an expecting mother, and found myself humming, doting on him. As if responding, he made my rapture more immense, stretching out my skin, my skin which was just a soft and thin film from which all this love could soon spill out.

I slept in my own private heaven that night, now and then woken only by the nervous thought that he would want to leave again.

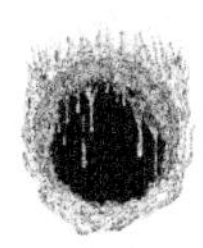

Thankfully, dad slept like a rock and heard nothing of the previous night's commotion. Rushing off to work, he even failed to notice me enraptured on the living room couch. I managed to get up, gather cleaning supplies, and rub off the streaks of dark brown I had left on the couch from sleeping in my ruined clothes. They came off with surprising ease. The stained bed sheets and torn pajamas were all tossed in the trash. Dad never asked a thing. Of the plants, he had nothing to add. It had been a long time since he had stopped looking at that corner that represented mom. It had been a long time since he stopped looking much at me, even.

At dinner the next night I ate very little. I grew to always feel full. Dad scraped the near-untouched steak into the trash bin and complained about the wasted food. Then, he only had one side-eye look at me, and his gaze fell on my stomach, covered by my outstretched shirt.

"Might be best, though, Dave," he said. "You're putting on a few pounds."

And that was that.

It may have been days. It may have been weeks. I lay in bed without doing anything else. I don't recall food. I don't recall dad having any questions. The clinking of dishes echoed outside my doorway one night. At least, I think it was nighttime—darkness had become a constant blanket. I guessed dad had brought me food which I did not want.

"I'm not playing this fucking game," he said, but then said no more.

I was lost. I was floating, light as smoke. My skin was velvet, eyes were limpid pools of a dark, dark water that never left. I rolled over once and noticed the hard plastic of the tarp I'd laid out on my bed after the sheets were ruined. It stuck to my back. I peeled it off in absentminded thought, not knowing how long I'd been blissfully asleep on it. As I rolled over, my limbs became ten times heavier. He wanted to sleep and could only do so when I did. He needed the machinations of my body relaxed down to a soft hum, so he kept me gorged on sweetness and narcotic joy. At one point I tried to force my eyes open, but it seemed there were no longer eyes there, only lids glued shut, all sight forever swallowed by the sumptuous black of his company.

So I slept for another day or two. In the constant drip and reverb of his generous loving, it felt like five lifetimes.

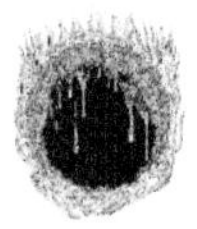

Twice more he left and fed. On his latest return, I knew there would soon be no space. It had felt like swallowing a boulder, firm and muscly, yet supple enough to contort and ball up so that eventually it managed to force itself back down, the blisters now as big as grapes.

The episodes without him were more hideous than ever. I could not stop shaking. I felt abandon settle inside every bone, and it stung and ached like a million fractures, like being ground down to bits. The exits no longer hurt. I had grown numb to that kind of pain, and only knew evidence of my injuries by how the brownish blood began to drip off the tarp I was sunk into. On his returns, I found I no longer needed food. With the life he stole elsewhere, he kept me fed and semiconscious as well. He also kept me happy, and that ecstasy *never* wore out. In dreams, he kept dancing as the tiny, gorgeous body I knew him as. Memory of the abscess-ridden thing died down. *This* was him, who loved to lather me in the echoes of his purity. *This* was him, laid out on my chest like the warmest, softest pound of flesh. The sedation was like silken fingers gently shutting my eyelids.

I was always smiling.

Only twice dad knocked at my door to check on me. The first check-in came in two faint knocks and a slight pause for response. I managed to say "I'm fine" in a gruff and broken voice, vocal cords frayed and gored from his returns. This was good enough for dad.

I figured on one outing he had fed on whatever insects he could find and grew to love the more nutritious taste of creatures livelier than plants. When dad knocked the second time asking where Jinx had gone, I knew what the second meal had been. I did not manage an answer and only heard a loud, retreating sigh in response.

I had no way of knowing how bloated I was. Pain no longer warned me. Pain was just *there*, a solid slab atop which the saccharine and deep-seeping pleasure settled. I knew there were stretchmarks like shallow gashes along my stomach. I knew saliva pooled at the back of my mouth and drooled out in thick, pinkish streams because it could no longer pass the throat. I knew every time he repositioned, my entire body twitched. The nerves could not respond to such an invasion. My stomach cried—I could only guess in pain—but it was ignored.

Because I was happy. Happiness itself managed to topple over trivial things like time and space, and it folded days upon days, and my bedroom and all the air in it became only like lukewarm water where my ever-still form floated. Again he sent the signals, hot air heavy with meaning and indescribable taste, but it was all now just one big word, the word that had always echoed:

"Love."

He *loved* me. Even through all the torture, he *loved* me. His feeding was only because he needed to stay alive, lest the heavenly single coil that now gave me this taste of ambrosia be severed forever and he perish inside me, starved.

He would not let that be.

Swollen, ready to burst with any stray kick of his claws, I hummed to myself, in mangled sounds, the subtle and private hymns that his beauty and adoration dictated.

He left again. A third time. He was so hungry. He screamed it at me. It still rang in my ears, an ugly voice I had never heard before. I was not ready for how brutal, how ravaging this last exit would be. My body screamed all over with a pain beyond the physical. It was a pain that scorched and scraped something in the gyri of my unconscious, a flaming kind of hurt where things should not ever be felt. I left my bed and dragged a trail of thick blood behind me. The loose skin of my stomach hung to my thighs. Arms outstretched, I only managed to stand on trembling legs because I needed to find him.

He had never been gone this long. Every second was a needle dug into the most tender part of myself, wherever that was. Every moment was like my warped organs being strangled by a rope made of fire.

I stumbled in darkness out of my bedroom and faintly looked around, reaccustoming to the use of my eyes. Dark, all dark, I only saw dark, and then a white door with a hole chewed out at its center.

Dad's door.

With just a faint air of realization, I sauntered over and opened it, knowing he would be in there.

The room seemed undisturbed, nothing out of place, as if even my dad had never been there. Yet, there he was, asleep on his bed, a calmness about him. I never knew he slept so peacefully. I guessed that with time, he had forgotten about mom, at least in dreams. Then the thought of mom came pounding, pounding, like a face vaguely familiar. Yes, there had once been mom. And now here was dad.

"Dad."

"Dad."

"Dad."

The word crawled over to me, tip-tapping until it made some sense.

I doubled over and vomited as the pain between my buttocks burned with an intensity that had been waiting for consciousness to let it seethe.

I was now at dad's side, not having perceived when I walked over to him. Now I was aware of my hands, how stained with shit and how frail they were. With a longing I had not felt in years, as if dad was a rescue boat after endless time at sea, after me drowning in the stinging, briny waters of forgetfulness, I reached out and caressed him.

His entire face crumbled and caved in under my shaking hand, turned to fine, fine dust. In my tenuous wakefulness, assured of being awake only by the constant pain all through my body, I had to force myself to realize I was not dreaming. The rest of dad's body followed. It all crumbled and sat as an ashy gray mound atop the bed sheets, drained of all life like mom's plants.

Just like mom's plants.

I nearly fainted, hitting the ground but still gingerly holding on to consciousness. Then I saw *it* emerge from the shadows, making a wet and scratchy sound as countless limbs now adorned its long, sinewy body roughly the size of a small child, speckled in blisters swollen and enormous, raw with greenish-white fillings. It spotted me agonizing on the floor, and the thought of dad and the vision of *it* as *it* was, as the monstrous, virulent, pustule-ridden slab of gristle that it was, all made me scream and retch. What little of my own energy I still had I used to crawl away from it in pathetic lunges.

I did not get far at all. It did not even approach me in any rush. Slowly, my jaws were opened. Even slower, it curled into shape, forcing its entry again. I felt the give of my front teeth as it pushed and pushed. I felt the sonorous snapping as my jaw dislocated.

In blood, mucus, and the viscous sweat it oozed, inch by grimy inch, it came back.

He came back.

And halfway through his return, when his front half had already touched something raw and sore inside me, when his teeth already chewed around to make his home more spacy and inviting, even with his rear end still at my lips, even with the familiar pus from burst blisters and the new, pulpy blood of my ruined gums, had my mouth not been stretched beyond its means into that gaping, inviting "O," I would have smiled.

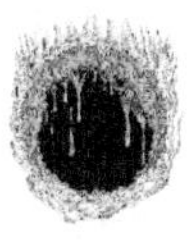

Now I'm fuller than I can be.

Now there's nothing living in this house except him and me.

Now he's hungry again.

Now the pleasure is indescribable. Now it doesn't even feel like pleasure. Now I don't know what pleasure could even be compared to so that it becomes pleasure. Pleasure is just a constant sleep. I am drowned in delectation, in a sickly hue that has deliquesced reality into the same mushy consistency of dreams. I don't have eyes. They're gone. I run my hands over my face, over my stomach, and it all comes away as dust.

Real dust.

It really *is* happening.

He's eating *me* now. There's no pain, just the sensation of once hard skin pulverizing, and then a final, cold teardrop running down my mealy face.

I never thought he would devour his own home, the very thing he promised so much love to. Maybe it's heartbreak that settles somewhere lost and hollow where a mind had once been, like muffled words through a closed mouth.

But that thought doesn't linger for long.

He knows what to do.

Even in the taste of rot and death at my failing lips, along the ruined, black hole where I think a mouth had once been—my mouth maybe—I feel the air of his language rise again, up my disfigured throat, and even in the last moments when my brain can still soak in the luscious privacy of his whispers, I feel the air escape and form into those beautiful words, and they're the last thing I feel before a darkness falls heavy on my sooty thoughts:

"Love."

"Love."

"Love."

HUNGER

The question of the evening was always, "what do you want for dinner?" He was still unsure of what she could and could not eat, and they were not going to go through another "sirloin steak with green beans" episode after she ended up half dead and ugly. It was always best to ask, to poke at her fancy, but not too much. Too much poking and Sal was sure he would find something unseemly. Dinner was enough as far as conversation went.

"Whatever you want," she responded in that needle-like voice. She had taken a fancy to that mystifying answer in recent days, only this once she inflected with a particular hiss, not loud enough to be hostile, but almost.

They both stared at each other, her one eye fixed on both of his. *Why do you do this to me?* Sal thought but did not say it. Still, even without saying it, he was unsure if she could read it in his eyes, or his face, or in other ways: The fact that he was uneasy, tired, and maybe more scared than he would ever admit. He was still unsure of a lot of things about her. It was scary, and it was not as fun as it had been before.

He finally settled on a large thin-crust pizza with mushrooms. *That* he was sure she could stomach, but it had been their dinner for a solid week now. It was the only thing he could remember her demanding and eating without bringing on the blisters, without bringing on the shedding skin falling on the bathroom tile with wet, stringy plops. Perhaps he should have paid more attention to her appetites back when she was receptive to his questioning, but it was too late now. He figured, by the way her many-fingered hand caressed every slice without eating, that she was somewhat displeased, but it was difficult to tell.

He tried to scrutinize those jittery fingers because her face said nothing; her porcelain-like, round, cold face, the one eye bloodshot and veneered in amberlike liquid, her mouth always settled into a thin smile. At least it *looked* like a smile. That expression only changed when it took things in. In those moments, the mouth twisted soundlessly into a perfect circle. Then she ate. Then it curled back into a little "v" and the jaws did not move, even though chewing sounds came out. Even when not particularly gleeful or pleased, she smiled. Even when annoyed, she smiled. He had never seen her sad or truly angry, but he was sure her expression would remain the same. He would not want to witness otherwise.

She went on caressing the pizza, digging pebble-like nails into the cooling cheese, staining them with sauce, like claws scratching flesh and drawing blood. He was not going to ask her to eat. Eventually she would eat as she saw fit. Hopefully. Right now she just watched him, but he paid no attention to it. Sal just then was more preoccupied by the pimply-faced delivery guy from earlier. He had driven away much too slowly after he had handed off their meal, and perhaps Sal had opened the door too wide, or maybe he had allowed the young man to linger for too long. He could tell the teen had looked over his shoulder, and Sal knew *she* was keen on always being close by. He did not know if she had been within the driver's sight, but he could tell the boy had let out a low "whoa" as he gawked over his shoulder. He was almost positive. Had he seen her, or had he whoa'd at something else? Was it all in Sal's head? Many things had been just in his head since her arrival, constant turmoil and worry at being unable to guess where she would move next, when she might slip out of the house and alert the neighbors, or when an unknown guest would surprise him and see them together. *It's not worth it*, he kept thinking. *It's not worth it even for* that.

Sal had then hurled out a $20 bill and bid the young guy goodnight, leaving him with an entire $8.50 tip. Shutting the door quickly, Sal immediately checked the little window next to it and watched. The boy had not lingered *too* long at the doorstep, but his slow drive away had been indeed suspicious. *Who'll believe a dumb fucking pizza guy?* He tried to ease his mind back at the dinner table. *Who'll believe a dumb teenager whose pizza uniform reeks of weed?*

He almost forgot about it, now refocusing back to her fingers dancing on the pizza, until she spoke once more. She was unusually chatty this evening.

"He saw."

Sal just stared at her, feeling cold sweat seeping through his forehead. His face almost twisted in horror, but he ironed it down back to indifference. He did not know why, but he did not like showing her his fear. *Why do you do this to me?* He thought again. But she was just bluffing. She *had* to be. She knew what was upsetting him, and she knew how to play with him. She had done it before.

Some moments passed and she finally stopped stroking. Her fur softened and stuck back down to her hide, and that is how he knew she was ready to eat. Slice after slice she stuffed nearly the whole thing down her gullet, chewing in perfect stillness, more rapidly than ever before. When she was done, there were two slices left on the grease-stained pizza box. The previous night she had only left one, and days before she had eaten through the whole thing. Her fur went back up, only this time it was not as pointed. It was soft, curling at the top, and it undulated serenely at the rhythm she commanded, showing impossible dexterity with every single one of her follicles. She was pleased. Heaven be blessed, she was *pleased*. Suddenly, the pizza boy didn't matter anymore. He recognized her signs. She was ready, inviting, making way for the next of their night affairs. The very movement of her hair was enough to get Sal hard, his erection pressing with painful pleasure against the crotch of his slacks.

Sal made his way to the bedroom, and she made no hesitation in following with slimy swiftness. The house was spacious, but he always did wonder why she chose to be nowhere else except near him, at every corner his eyes darted over to, like a shadow that may or may not be illusion until he fixed his gaze intently at her. It seemed she *demanded* attention. It seemed she wanted him to always know she was there. On this particular night, she seemed to take great pleasure in his absentminded torment, and had she really said, "He saw"? But that affair seemed to be over, her motions and bristling calling for finality.

That pizza boy said "whoa" because he probably remembered some stupid joke. Maybe he was too high or too dumb to say anything else. That boy didn't see shit.

And thus came the end of the night. With every step leading upstairs, Sal grew more relaxed, slowly unbuttoning the top buttons of his shirt, then a few more steps and his belt came unbuckled, and then at the entrance of their bedroom his shoes came off.

His bedroom.

As he gathered some composure by leaning on the doorframe, she swept past him and made herself comfortable at the foot of his bed. She curled into a ball, dark and featureless under the cover of night, save for some icy spots of moonlight peeking through the blinds. They fell on her and only revealed slivers of brown and green. She had buried her face into herself, and now she waited.

Sal finished undressing slowly and with shame. "It's been a long day," he said, more to himself than to her, more so to justify what was coming, perhaps, as if saying he *really* needed this. Indeed it had been quite a long and painful day, and indeed he needed this. In fact, every day was long, plagued with the smell of hot printer ink and the feeling of plastic keyboard keys under the tips of his fingers; long days of editing boilerplate Court motions of this and that, filing and copying, half-reading transcripts of people talking about things he did not care about. Days of numbed movement, of tasteless talk and sterile thinking with people as tired and unamicable as him. He only wanted to come to *her* at night. For those past two sweet and tender months since she had arrived, it was all he thought about. But not the "her" that was hungry for food, evasive and mercurial; not the taunting "her" that knew how to push buttons and say just the things to make his stomach turn.

No.

He wanted the "her" that was there right now, waiting for him, hungry for *him*. Though shapeless and monstrous, she gestured in ways that were submissive, thrown to passion, giving in to his will and power, tickling at the darkest, most unknown of his fancies, things of his body and mind that no one else but her could taste and relish. She wanted him, and just the way he wanted her to want him.

Still, he undressed with shame, the way a little boy scurries back inside his house after he's done something wrong. As if caught with stolen candy in his hands or dirt and mud on his Sunday best, he came naked into his own bedroom looking downward as she unburied her sight from her curled position and turned to face him.

"Come," she whispered icily, and her words were as heavy and sedative as the night. Sal moved forward in little shy steps. The carpet was smooth against his bare feet, still sore from being mushed inside his Oxfords all day long. The air was cool as it seeped in through the inch-long opening of the window, hitting his naked body and the folds of his heavy skin that had been boiling under the layers of his business casual. After so many hours at the office, it felt wrong to have the outside elements lick his nude body so, but then it felt right. His mind was now composed, melting into the mood of the scene. He walked with purpose towards her. She extended a thick strand of hair, and it curled around his leg without him noticing, until it started tickling, making him fully erect. Her thick, coarse threads made the hairs on his leg feel like peach fuzz. He kept walking, awkwardly now that she pulled his one leg forward. Soon, their bodies met, and her mouth changed shape, into that solid "O" as it readied to receive him. Sal's arms dangled helplessly at his sides, no longer in control, not wanting to touch her, but giving in to her, nonetheless. She took him in, and her insides were soft and perfect and sweet. It was just as he liked it.

Sal closed his eyes. He always tried to close his eyes first. The movements of the thin tissue of her gullet worked to bring him back to that first time. It was always what he thought of, being a child, finding the pressure of the water pump as he swam to the corner of his parents' swimming pool, where they could not see him even if they came out to the backyard canopy. His head half-submerged, he found the pressure of the water tickling his stomach, and then he floated up a bit, so it hit him *there*. Then, pathetically thrusting his untrained hips, he had felt the pressure of the water hit him *there* again as it pushed him back while he pushed forward. There he had remained for some slow seconds, not knowing what he wanted but knowing he wanted it, and that he could reach it the more it tickled and then it wasn't just tickling anymore. When it reached, like *she* made him reach, his body shivered from head to toe, and hurled back to the present he grabbed the bedpost with trembling hands just as his hands back then had balled into fists against the tiled insides of the pool, and then he cried out more so than moaned. Back in the pool it had been clean and swift, but back in his bedroom, he made a mess of himself. She, however, ate it all, sucked it in and relished it with pleased clicking noises, all the cum ejecting from him and all the sweat that drenched him. Like a vacuum, she worked her gullet all over him, catching every bead of perspiration with quenchless thirst, feeling her move around places even he seldom felt on himself. That cold hole ran against his armpits, against the back of his ears, against the nape of his neck and in between his toes, working with fearsome speed while he was still panting from his orgasm. Then she worked her way down on him again and readied herself, wanting to take him in again.

He had to softly push her back. "Wait," he said in a childlike whimper, barely keeping his knees from buckling, upset that he had to lay his hands on her during such an intimate part of his feelings. She didn't feel right to the touch when he was still thinking about the time in the pool.

She seemed to understand and stood perfectly still. He looked at her briefly, and she was back to being the ugly, monstrous thing with no shape. His head started pounding as he made for the bed. Lying there, still naked, he was spent and felt his stomach turning. She still waited at the foot of the bed, not moving, as she had been left. His dick felt raw, flaccid, not a single thought of pleasure in his mind. He threw his arm over his eyes, wanting to forget it, perhaps forget the whole ordeal of the night, perhaps forget *her* entirely.

Yet, his nakedness only reminded him of it all, and it had *really* been a painful, torturous, suffocating day at work. His nakedness was relief by default, and he started running his hands up and down himself. Soon enough, with the soft linen against his bare buttocks and his bare thighs, he was hard again, harder than before, more frustrated than before. It took him only minutes to not think again.

"Come," only this time he said it, and he heard the viscous serpentine thing unfold itself and scurry to the side of the bed to join him. She had somehow shrunk, the imposing mass of bristled quills gorging at the dinner table now only as big as his leg, and softer, tickling and then not tickling but still feeling good to his skin. "How do you do that?" he asked out loud in a surprised moan, but he could tell she was not listening.

This time she took her time, was not as forceful, as if understanding he was in the mood for tenderness now. For what seemed ages, the two bodies lay curled on each other, this time in simultaneous passion, his hips thrusting and her head bobbing with a shared rhythm. She never let go of him, and he now wrapped his arms around her down-like pelt and closed his eyes, not forcefully shut, but half-squinted. Now he didn't think of the time in the pool. Now it was here, now, and she felt good to the touch. She undulated. He felt her skin under the fur, cold and scale-like. He felt her muscles, turgid and boneless, something like a heartbeat slapping against his bare chest, against his own excitement. He *fucked* her. He fucked *it*. Those were his last thoughts, and then he smiled with pleasure. He shuddered, and his mind turned to fleece.

And then she ate again.

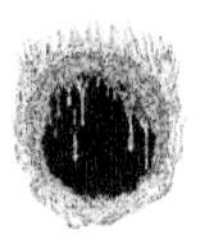

"Yeah, mom, she's cute," Sal shouted into the receiver. "I don't know her, though. What if she's a meth head like the last one?"

His mother said something else, but he didn't listen, only noted that she did not laugh. He only said "yes" and "have to go" and hung up as he tied his tie. Thank fuck she didn't know his cell number. Mom was always thinking of a girl for Sal, any girl she saw and did small talk with, any girl who showed faint interest at the supermarket whenever she announced that she had a single son with a good salary and a nice home in the so-so part of town. Sal had at first been unyielding yet feigning interest, but now he was simply dismissive. He could not possibly need any girl his mom deemed right for him.

That morning she had not followed him downstairs as he readied for work. It was always 50/50. Sometimes she stayed in the bedroom until nighttime, others she came down to watch him in silence. He liked her in the bedroom more. He could pretend she did not live there, and he was glad to have the quiet morning to take in the lower story of the house, the bland breakfast, and the hours away from the office, half-listening to an audiobook on his headphones, staring out the window into nothing. There was a long day ahead, with cut personnel, and with the head lawyer of the firm having implored him to "make sacrifices" as they all had. Taking on the workload of Charlie and Shawn, he thought of quitting, moving away, living off the fat of the land somewhere that may or may not exist, somewhere in Idaho—that state always sounded right for isolation, though he had never been. He then wondered if he would take *her*. He had no answer for that. He then chose not to dwell on it anymore and instead gulped down the cooling coffee and nibbled on some toast before he was late.

She would not want to eat until evening. She fed only once a day. Or twice, depending on how Sal thought to view it. Right now, she did not exist, *did not exist*. The mantra trembled on his lips, and he thought of the time before she had arrived.

It was mixed. It was complicated, like everything. He still longed for that loneliness, *but that was unfair to her after all she had done for him*. (This last thought made him chuckle. He could not believe such a thing had crossed his mind. *Unfair to her!*) If only she could vanish, just for a while, just when she wasn't needed, existing only at night. Those early days, after she had shown up at his doorstep and scurried in as he opened the door, had been the best. How startled he had been, shocked out of his mind and with 911 ready at hand. Then she had approached, softly, loosening and touching him. She had been shy, mistrusting, only unfurling in pleasure when she felt safe enough. She had even seemed cute, a lost little lamb looking for a shepherd, a little child looking for daddy. She had been reassured enough by his words, "I won't hurt you" as he had pulled his pants down. It was as if she knew what she was good for, what she could do and do it well. She had choked at first ("too big for you?" he had said, the words making him feel powerful, oppressive, as he had never felt before), but after that magical first touch they had shared, it was as if she had been made *for* him. Then he found she could talk, could eat, in fact *demanded* conversation and food, and demanded *him*. Once she had loosened and started to demand *him*, it had been the most ecstatic throw into bliss. And from that day she had earned her spot in the house.

But maybe it had been much too quick. Now she could not be washed off. Now with her glares, with her teasing, with her unpredictability, her picky tastes... Now it was not as fun.

Then the "sirloin steak with green beans" incident happened. He remembered how he had planned for their romantic dinner under candlelight, expensive steak cooked to perfection, and as she opened up to take the dripping meat in, she had made a sound he had never heard before, something like a blender mixed with a dying bird, projectile vomiting the meal and then past meals, past nights with him, melted cheese and half-chewed chunks of meat and yellowed, semi-hardened globs of semen strewn across his dining room floor, forever staining his expensive sheepskin rug as she erratically wobbled to the living room, her fur turning a faded lilac, shedding, exposing skin that fell to the touch, skin that reeked of putrid fruit. The clean-up... That's when things had stopped being pure bliss. From then on he knew she needed maintenance. She could react in unforeseen ways. Somehow, up until then, he had never wondered much about her origin and had simply welcomed her and her willingness to give pleasure. Then, like a brick to his head, he realized he did not even know what she was, or what she really wanted, or why she was there.

He did not like that.

Deciding that that was way too much recollection, sad and foreboding, Sal finished his breakfast and headed for the door. Just then, however, she was suddenly there at the foot of the staircase, having descended without a sound, as if materialized from thin air, her stone face pointed at him.

"I'm off to work," he thought to say to her, not knowing why, not knowing if she even understood.

She was unmoved.

Before he could step back out of reflex, she was at him, undoing his zipper with seven excited, worming fingers. "Now," she kept repeating in a high-pitched purring. "Now, now, now."

"Stop it!" Sal shouted, almost saying *please* before catching himself. "I have to go! I'm going to be late!" He was scared. She had never asked for anything in the mornings. With shaking hands he pushed her back but didn't fight hard enough. He was hard again. Then, he was still pushing her, but now it was playful. Now he smiled. "You really want it now, don't you?" he said without thinking, his voice lower, more relaxed, invigorated by being desired. Finally, his arms went limp at his sides, his lower body bent towards her. He repeated, “Stop it! I have to go!” But he was fully in her.

And he liked this game.

She took him in as she had never done during morning hours. The cover of night was gone, and for the first time, they did it while he saw her fully, in broad daylight. Her once sensuous, tendrilous movements in the dark were now revealed as the long and contorting hairy thing she was. He shut his eyes once he caught her rhythm, the “O” shape of her mouth shrinking and gripping him with strength. He did not feel that recollection of childhood pleasure he often felt at night, no thoughts of being a kid at the pool. This time it was blunt, felt good, but only like scratching an itch.

Suddenly, he felt burning pain explode from his crotch down to his loins. She was gripping, tighter and tighter, and something like a sharp tooth which he had never felt before jutted out from her gullet, scratching the head of his dick like the prong of a fork pressing down against his softening flesh.

“Stop!” he screamed with agony, really meaning it now, pushing her back, but she did not care this time. She remained latched, and now with her new denture began a soft chewing that broke through his skin.

Sal balled his hands into tight fists and struck her, softly at first from the shock, then with full force once he recognized the real threat, the blows bouncing against her soft body, unsure whether he was causing any damage or not, unsure if she could even feel pain. His mind racing, face hot and twisted with pain and anger, he burst into panic and began to scream, panic over what she would do to him, having him so fully in her grasp, fists raining down, some punches missing, but most landing. Eventually she undid her bite and scurried away, drooling out a sound like hurt crying.

Chest heaving up and down, pants around his ankles, Sal leaned against the front doorframe, perspiration already building up and staining his button-up shirt, cold sweat soaking through the pits and collar. Before he knew it, he was smiling, lowering one hand to check his genitals, smiling that it was all still there—wet, raw with pain, but there. He smiled with relief, but also smiled at her crying sound, knowing he could hurt her, knowing she really *was* vulnerable. She was as vulnerable as any creature, like a penitent dog. He looked up and saw her, back to her small stature, curled up, her eye intent on him. Then he saw the absence on her face. Her smile was gone. Her mouth altogether was gone, as if it had never been there, as if her lips closed off into seamless halves like a perfectly shaved rock being put back together. The two stared into each other. What was this new expression? What was she thinking? Had she known pain before this moment?

She must know now, he thought, *that I'm stronger*.

"Don't fucking do that!" He yelled out, surprised at the still simmering anger in his voice, pointing an accusatory finger as one scolds a child. "Don't you ever fucking do that again! It's only when *I* want it, okay? It's only when *I* fucking want it!"

He thought to leave at that moment, storm off into his car and forget the entire thing happened, but for some reason, it occurred to him to wait for an answer from her, like an angry parent who wishes to hear true regret in their scolded guilty child's voice.

Slowly uncurling, her fur disheveled from the beating (and Sal could see under the fur her skin was starting to bruise, stained with dark violet), she made her jittering fur dance, moving every follicle but slowly, carefully. Even in this obscure language, he understood. She was being submissive and being understanding. She had recognized the boundaries being drawn. There was something lowered and disarmed about the way she moved.

Then, as if to seal everything, she spoke, in a tone so sweet that he had never heard from her before.

"Okay," she replied.

By reflex, moved by her meekness, he nodded, and made his way to his car after pulling up his pants, wincing at the pain around his crotch which still burned and would burn for a while.

They had struck an understanding, a mutual agreement. He continued to smile to himself, but now with a serenity washing over him. He had controlled her. He had won. As he buckled up in his car seat and began his commute, he never once thought to look back to check on her. He even forgot the attack, for a real breakthrough had come of it.

And he could hurt her.

In his rush, Sal was unable to see her still lurking in that same corner, the chewing and slurping sounds coming from beneath her face, relishing every drop of blood she had been able to draw.

It was a taste she liked.

Back at the dinner table that night, Sal still simmered from the day at work. That miserable, wretched, fucked, piled-shit-of-a-day at work thanks to Roger, the uppity junior lawyer who had entered that office as a snot-nosed paralegal, but as soon as he had passed the bar exam with high marks he had started shitting out more money than Sal could ever dream of with his beginners' luck settlements. Of course Roger had been the one to notice and point down to his stained crotch. It had set off his famous jeering, shit-eating grin in full display as he proclaimed,

"You didn't do enough shaking there, Sal," and patted him on the shoulder as if it were all friendly banter among pals. Sal almost recoiled from his touch but held it together. Then, all three nearby secretaries had their eyes drawn to his pants, a quarter-sized darkened blotch staining his khaki slacks near his dick, not wet with piss, but with blood. He hadn't even noticed she had drawn blood until then. When he checked before clocking in, he had only found swollen skin too painful to touch or wipe. Smiling, he buried himself behind his desk, wordless, face burning with anger and shame, wanting to smash Roger through a window, wanting to slice his neck open with a letter opener. Only Roger had laughed, but they had all seen, and they all had looked ashamed—ashamed for him, pitying him.

Then there had been the flurry of calls from angry clients (and when would he be able to afford his own fucking secretary to sift through these low lives for him? Never), clients demanding the Court magically move faster, demanding miracles out of their open-and-shut cases, demanding that he undo all their piss-poor choices, assuage their innate lack of judgment. Connie McGuire in particular, that meth-head cunt, was driving him up a wall. She had been caught with some illegal brass knuckles and would really only have to do some community service and get a move on with her miserable life. Yet she was still appealing the guilty verdict, wasting the Court's time, the same Court that already had a short temper for Sal, as he always seemed to get stuck with the biggest idiots. She was blowing up on the phone that day, demanding he look over the same fucking law again ("Yup, it's still illegal for you to be a fuckwit, Connie," he wanted to scream), find some magic fucking words in the Declaration of Independence that would proclaim "By golly, she's innocent after all!" Then he heard her tone change through the phone speaker, could just picture her gaunt, bone-dry face lighting up in a condescending smile that had no business condescending anything as she pointed at him, her tinny, drawling voice saying, "*You* work for *me*, buddy, so do your fucking job right!" Forget stepping on shit. He was being stepped on *by* shit all day long.

Then he noticed, back at the dinner table, that his breathing had gotten heavy, his fists were tightened, and he glared directly at *her*, without seeing her, seeing past her at a red-hot image of Roger and Connie bleeding out, a bundle of twisted and fat-covered guts flowering before him, him gazing with a delight that would never actualize. His expression softened, regarding her and her long, griseous body, bruises magically healed, fur back to its pristine, combed-down state, as if nothing had happened (just like the "sirloin steak with green beans" incident—she was resilient for sure), and he read, perhaps selfishly, a willingness from her part to forget (*Selfishly*? These sympathetic thoughts towards her continued to mystify him). In this cool moment, slowly dragging himself down from his ire, he regarded her with a stomach-turning, tender feeling he would have thought impossible before.

She had hurt him, and he had hurt her, but now they broke bread in peace, and had she not been the only thing to reward him with any kind of pleasantness that entire day? As he had walked through the door, feet dragging, having forgotten about her entirely, sifting through the three voicemails mom had left that day without a goddamned actual thing to say ("Just wanted to check in on you," "What did you decide about Regina's daughter?" "Oh, your father keeps telling me to stop bothering you"), *she* had scurried down, keeping a respectful distance, and had fixed her eye on him, in an expression much more human than he had ever seen. As if having read his mind the previous day (*and could she actually?*), attuned to his prior frustrations over her indecisiveness, wanting a truce, she had stated in a delicate and direct voice, "Thin-crust pizza with mushrooms."

Straight to the point, no more fucking around. They understood each other now: He would feed her, and then he would feed her again.

The same pimply pizza boy had arrived, but this time she had had the good conscience to stay out of sight. The boy seemed to have forgotten the previous night's events entirely, possibly did not even recall he had been to the same house every night for the past week. As he sat down to eat with her, her with her pizza and him with a bagged salad, they ate in what he would describe as peaceful, *homely* silence. Now she was done, and her mouth had resettled into its usual smile, some pizza grease dripping at its sides. This time, however, she had left half the pizza untouched.

He wondered what to do, and then, without thinking, he raised from his seat and walked to her side, picked up a *Tony's Pizza*-branded napkin from the table and tenderly cleaned up the grease staining her face. His stare was blank, not wanting to acknowledge his action, but hoping she would recognize he was reciprocating their civil understanding. Her hair pulsated quietly. She seemed to enjoy that touch, perhaps.

Connie fucking McGuire, Roger, that shit-eating bastard, his own mother that couldn't keep her fucking mouth shut. He hated it all. He was humiliated, exhausted, needed that release. Even his own mother, he admittedly to himself now—he wanted to bash her skull in. *Stupid, nosy bitch.* A burning sensation overtook him, a hot flush of shame at finally having to acknowledge it: Since her arrival, he looked forward, every night, only to his release through *her.* It was all he ever wanted, all that made him feel that deep, gripping, ensnaring pleasure, all that stress and anger uncoiling from his innards and spewing out for her to receive, for her to relish. And *she* wanted it. She wanted his anger, his acrid release, every one of his liquids. She looked forward to it, too.

He finished cleaning her. Even with all the grease and heavily garlicked sauce, she never smelled, never had bad, off-putting breath (not even when it all had come spewing back out), as if she ate up and digested every single molecule that went in her, even the scents. Her insides were a mystery, a void that received, and dangerously, evidently, she sometimes refused to let things back out. She was hungry, so, so hungry, that she left no room even for waste. She either never left behind any droppings, or she did a good job at hiding them. He had never found anything.

"I..." he started, then hesitated, unsure if she would understand how imposing and commanding he wanted to be, how much control he wanted to exert, and how it was part of his pleasure now. He was unsure if she would know, after their earlier altercation, and her eventual relenting, that he had been looking forward to uttering these words to her all day, tasting them in his mouth with saccharine longing for every waking hour at work. "I want it now. I want it now."

With no hesitation, she made her way to the bedroom, leaving him behind. He sat there a moment by himself, wondering what was happening, stupefied, angry at himself for being so dependent. How had she managed to undo all his rage just like that? He had wanted to sound commandeering. Instead he had sounded pathetic, desperately begging. Still, he sauntered on, following her path.

Once more they were in bed together. She did not hungrily move on him like previous nights, but awaited further instruction, on her own side of the bed, curled up, very different from that viscid, serpentine thing that had lunged towards him that morning, obscene in its clarity. She was back to her darkened self, and with an added note of submission, even helplessness, in the way she curled and fluffed her hair. Sal finished undressing, fully nude and hard, and slipped under the covers next to her. Her silhouette was almost human. He had made sure to shut the blinds entirely this time, so that next to him was only another living thing, half his stature and covered in fur, but with a heartbeat, soft noises brewing from within like regular human breathing.

"Do you know what this is called?" He asked her in a soft voice, resisting the urge to caress her, not knowing why. "What we do every night, do you know what it is?"

She said nothing. He felt her body grow warmer, fully tremble. Was this how she showed anticipation, excitement? Or did it mean something else?

"It's fucking," he said, feeling a delight in instructing, teaching her, perhaps corrupting her. He did not know if she knew prudishness. She had arrived knowing English but had never once cussed or been vulgar. Thinking on it, she had never said much. "We're going to fuck. *I'm* going to fuck you."

Grabbing her by the nape of the neck, delicate yet firm, he guided her head to his crotch. She did not resist. He closed his eyes, bit his lip, and let her do the rest. She was swifter now, desperate, wanting his release. He knew it. His legs wrapped around her. His toes curled. All went light down there, feeling pleasant and powerful like nothing else ever did.

Then he came inside her, had no time to think back to the pool, or anything else, simply engaged in that moment with her, mind as dark as the room, her body, and her thoughts. With toes uncurling, he let her eat all over, once more consuming all the sweat, every crease explored with that faint suction, hungry, persistent, more than ever before.

Then he heard the wet, tearing sound of his flesh coming undone before he even realized what was happening. Her cold, fork-like teeth had latched on to his neck just then. At once he was pulling her off of him, and in that pulling motion, a thin strip of his skin went along with her like a red worm, red even in the dark, dangling from her mouth, stripped off from the end of his jaw to his collarbone, a straight line down. Things came alive with pain and the warm smell of blood, the taste of sulfur as it splashed around his lips, the warmth of it curling down to the back of his neck and staining the bed sheets and pillowcase. He managed to sock her straight in the eye before she retreated to the corner of the room. It had felt like hitting raw meat, shaved and wet as she went scurrying, letting out a shrill screech that pierced through his ears.

Stumbling to the bathroom, he was strangely efficient: first-aid kit, pressure applied, alcohol that stung all the way to the inside of his throat. He tried to hold his blood and frayed skin in shape as tight as possible, working to the soft beat of his blood hitting the white porcelain sink in small but persistent drops. It was an ugly, adrenaline-soaked fear taking over him, anxiety crashing in and out like maddened waves even as his hands worked with dexterity, wrapping gauze around his neck like a choker. He was afraid, side-eying the shut bathroom door of the master bedroom, looking to see if she might be trying to slip in, might even try to break the door down, hungry for another taste. *How strong is she?* Sal wondered, worried that the door might not hold. But there was nothing, only silence once he managed to get himself back in shape.

Stepping cautiously back outside, adjusting his eyes to the darkness, he cursed himself for not having hit the light switch on his way to the sink. However, the bathroom light was enough to make out a rough shape of his surroundings, and he saw her. She was in the same corner she had escaped to, curled up, hair bristled, pointing straight up. *Is she ready to attack?* He made his presence known, fully stepping out of the bathroom doorframe, within her range of vision, but she made no movement. It seemed she was frozen, could even be a pile of clothes tossed carelessly aside, but the hairs were unmistakable.

Before he knew it, he was at her, kicking with all his strength. His hits landed in hollow claps and thuds like breaking the surface of water, tearing out handfuls of her fur that seemed to soften and dissolve like cotton candy once they came undone from her follicles. Her screams were loud, eerily womanlike, equally scared as his grunts and pants, but he never worried about the neighbors hearing. They knew to mind their business anyway. Soon, the punches became wet with her blood, her ooze, clear and brownish, and now he was stomping at her like she was a cockroach, back to being that unwanted pest he had wanted out of his house that morning.

"Fuck you!" he kept screaming, genuine hurt in his voice, betrayal breaking up his vocal cords. "Fuck you, you fucking cunt, fuck you!"

She never fought back.

He stormed out, jammed the door from the outside with a nearby stool, and noticed his barely scabbing wound was now bleeding through the gauze and aching more than before. He chose to only apply gentle pressure with his hand for the remainder of the night, having left all the gauze in the bathroom, in there with her. Just then he noticed he was still nude, but his arousal was gone. He was cold, mildly shivering, heart pounding loudly in his temples as he pressed his ear against the bedroom door like a nude, weak, vulnerable child checking to see if his parents were still mad. She did not cry any longer. It was the sound of an empty bedroom.

He grabbed some discarded shorts from the long-desolate guest bedroom and headed downstairs, making a crude bed on the sofa with some linen from a storage cabinet. With two aspirins from the kitchen, he lay down and tried to sleep. Somehow, the silence upstairs was more unnerving than any noise she could make. Then, he noticed he had barely blinked since she had done that to him. His eyes were dry, sore, jittering in their sockets.

It was not fun anymore.

He was scared.

Still holding his neck, still soaked with lukewarm blood, he shut his eyes tight, like a kid wishing an imaginary demon to go away. “Please,” he said in his softest voice. “Please, go away.”

He cried himself to sleep.

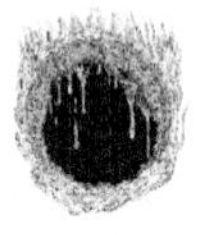

She chewed, swallowed, her mouth that thin smile once more, savoring. Every bit of her inside gullet was a taste bud, relishing that new taste she had discovered, pulpy and fibrous, thin and chewy. *Flesh from him.*

The hunger was immense, an ache all throughout, her entire body an empty stomach yearning for more. His blows had only registered as hollow impressions from the outside, the way one hears a muffled conversation from a shut door. All was distant, ghostly, bordering on nonexistence, but still she had felt the danger, for he really could kill her. So she had retreated. It was no matter. What mattered was what went inside her, and what she had tasted that night had been the most pleasing, heavenly thing she had ever passed.

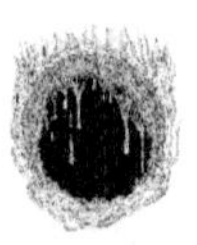

The next morning, with barely any sleep, Sal dared to open the bedroom door. He would not be scared by her, he had decided, although his hands still trembled. Back in his bedroom, reclaiming his territory, damn near pissing all over the carpet in defiance, he eyed her only in passing, as if to show her she had not shaken him. She was still in the same corner, as if during all those hours she had not moved a single inch. Indeed, that seemed to be the case. Nothing was out of order. There were no scratches on the door. She had made no attempts at escaping.

Undoing his bandages, he noticed the wound was bigger than he had imagined. It would leave a hideous scar, and right at that moment it was a soft pink, deep violet bruising all around it, like a partly peeled fruit revealing humid pulp underneath. He applied new bandages and dressed in a rush, pulling unmatching business casual attire from its hangers. Luckily, he remembered to also check the shoebox in the corner of the closet. From it, he pulled an old .44 Special his father had given him long ago for home security. "Dad, I'm not a psycho," he had told him, tucking it away in the dark for years. Here he was now, tucking it away in his pants, for some reason making sure she did not see. Would she know what it was? Or at the very least, would she know what his intentions were? He had never ascertained whether or not she could read minds.

He rushed downstairs and missed his breakfast. He was running late. There would be no way to hide the wound or the thick bandage around it, but at that moment nothing from work was of any concern. Even in such a hurry, he thought to check the revolver's chamber, carefully eyeing its orifices.

He had two bullets.

He hoped she would only need one.

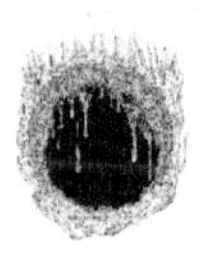

She knew he would die, and so would she. She knew how much she had hurt him. Even that was evident, by the way he had reacted. He had reacted the same when she had her first taste. This was the one thing she could not eat.

Forbidden fruit, always the sweetest.

She felt the dull bruises he had left on her already healing, but it would take more food to fully heal, and he was the only provider. Eat him, and there would be nothing more. She would starve after he was done. She would waste away.

Still, she *had* to. It tasted too good to pass up. Just the thought of being engulfed in it made her ache and ache with longing. Her stoic face belied the chaos of her undulous tripes and innards, her pain that sifted out in an exalted hair-dance, a dance like drooling, like savoring.

But he was strong, so it had to be through his means. He would have to be eased into it. She would play his game once more.

She would eat fully that night.

On the drive back home, Sal's mother called. She had finally gotten dad to give her his cellphone number. Dad was always a pushover in the end.

"Sweetie?"

"Yes, mom?"

"Oh, I just thought I'd call. Do you remember—"

"Mom, before you go on, I want to tell you something."

"What's that, dear?"

"Go fuck yourself."

And that had been that, how he had lost everything in a day, from the moment he had felt Roger's nose crush under his fist like a thin nutshell as soon as he had teased, "That's a new way to hide your hickeys, huh, buster?" He wished he had crushed his goddamned face before he could finish his shitty little joke.

He barely remembered spitting on the head attorney's face before he could ask what the fuck was going on.

His only regret was that he didn't do more. He had not tossed everything out of its place. He had not smashed his computer in. He had not broken anybody else's nose. By the time security had been called in, he was already driving back home. And now his mom, speechless at last, hung up the phone on her end.

Parked in his driveway, he started to cry. It was fear again. *Now you cry, you fucking pussy,* he teased himself. *What are you crying for now, you fucking faggot? What's that gonna do now?* He hadn't cried in so long, and now he had cried two days in a row. And just how everyday his thoughts slowly unwound from day-to-day life to refocus on what was at home, at this moment, he remembered.

It was all because of *her*.

He stormed into the house and found her, as usual, waiting for him at the bottom of the stairs. He raised the revolver, pointing straight at her eye. He figured a bullet through that soft opening would do it.

She did not flinch. She did not fear his movement, his intent. She couldn't read minds after all.

Yet, he hesitated. His finger trembled, not even daring to touch the trigger. He was soaked in sweat, bloodshot eyes not daring to look directly at her. Now he was crying for a third time, a deep feeling of longing in his gut, something lost and touch-starved and unable to nourish itself. He held a hand to his belly. Stomach aches, like when mom and dad were still at work and there was no food at home.

He might as well go through with it. There would be charges pressed. He would be disbarred. He would lose the house. They would find *her*. Who knew what would follow from there?

He readied his finger.

"Do you want it now?" she asked.

The revolver dropped from his hand.

Her words had entered him, medicinal, through every receptive orifice of his body, all his anger splayed out, so that he felt carved out, weightless, dropping to his knees, burying his face in his hands. She moved closer, as if sensing his need for touch, his need to be acknowledged. Even in the light, she was not entirely unseemly. She had fully healed from his earlier beating. Her smile had not faltered. She was focused on him, soft, bringing peace. *As always*.

"I'm sorry," he muttered. "It's been a long day."

She turned briefly to the side, eyeing the gun. Did she know? How much could she deduce? Her mind was always a mystery, but for the first time, he was curious. He wanted to pry. He wanted to connect. Still, he asked nothing.

She was the one to break the silence. "Do you want it now?" she repeated.

He did not know how to respond and still thought of reaching for the gun. His tears were stopped now in pure bewilderment, eyes shut in deep thought that was going nowhere, only in circles, in a woozy flurry that made him feel even lighter. Then he thought of how he was saving that other bullet for Connie fucking McGuire, for Roger, for his mom...

For himself. He had finally thought it should be for himself.

That's when he noticed her hairs were upon him, soft and clumsily feeling him up like a child's searching, curious hands, reaching around his waist, gently caressing where she had left the wound on his neck and playfully touching his belt buckle, moving anxiously but delicately, slowly making her way down to his crotch.

He was hard again.

"Do you want it now?" she asked a third time.

His mouth was hanging open, slowly gasping. "Yes," he said with hot breath, but it was more like she squeezed it out of him. Another bundle of hairs had worked around his shoulders, gently massaging them. It felt good. It felt so good. It was the best thing he had felt in years.

His hands were on her then. He reciprocated, massaged, played with the hair, wondering where her erogenous zones were. Then he thought to run a finger gently around her mouth. Her hair tightened at this touch, contracted, and he heard a soft, delicate, beautiful moan emerge from within her. He kissed her where her cheek would have been. He kissed her all over, licked her body, tasting something rotten but nurturing, nibbling her hair as she continued rubbing him. His hands were relentless, but her body was his to do as he pleased. Running his hands all over, wanting her softer, smaller, the entire serpentine, lurching thing around him. "I want you," he moaned, feeling her hairs wrap around the head of his dick. "I want you," he kept begging.

"I want you," she replied.

There had been no time for pizza as they rushed to the bedroom.

She was starving.

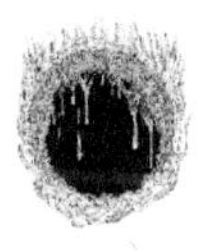

For the first time he felt her nakedness, too. They were wrapped around each other, fingers locked, his ten with her many, his chest hair a thin set of shavings against her muscular, furry pelt that felt like downy feathers and coarse wire at the same time. He had been in her for a long time, eyes half-shut, lost in pleasure, relishing every moment.

She worked him arduously, and he let her. His hips were glued down to the bed under her weight. She was imposing, massive, bigger than she had been before. He was close, edging on that orgasm, his entire groin ablaze with lively, tickling bliss.

He knew when she tasted it, she would want more. That's how she had decided to get a taste from his neck. Was he really ready to let her?

Before he knew it, he had already come, and her hunger was voracious, unrelenting, digging in deeper and deeper, those fork-like teeth slowly jutting from her soft, heavenly gums.

He did not think about how much it would hurt this time—how much it was already hurting; how much she had already eaten through him. Her chewing was slow, relishing, but persistent, and every bit she ate was like an ounce of pain being lifted from him but leaving behind its scorched nestling place.

And she had yet to chew so much, had yet to find the delectable texture of his tendons, the fat and rich pleasure of his muscles, and the cold and rigid delight of his bones, but she would soon get there. It was the most pain he had ever felt in his life, and yet his arms hung limply at his sides, and her let her, and it was like he was stuck in that orgasm for long, sultry years.

It was both of their hungers they were feeding that night.

ACKNOWLEDGMENTS

Like crazed litanies, I'm going to rattle off the people who helped make a hole in my head big enough for this book to squeeze through:

Thank you to James and Carmina, for fostering my love for reading and writing throughout my most impressionable and difficult years.

Thank you to the friends I have known since middle school: Olympia, Brianda, José, Dilan, Gilberto, Ricardo, and Erick. Your constant presence, either at the margins or fully embroiled in the constant tug-and-pull of my life, has been a pillar.

Thank you to Jay, for the continued reassurance that I'm not the only mess of a human going through it.

Thank you to the Masked Wonder of Pennsylvania, Parts Unknown, for the added encouragement, both in writing and life.

Thank you to Cameron Chaney, for inspiring me to pick this torture we call writing back up.

Thank you to Brendan Vidito, for providing the initial feedback and encouragement I needed to convince myself this is worth a damn.

Thank you to Merel, for the early help in making sense of some of these word tunnels.

Thank you to Indrid, for the wonderful art that really arrived at the soul of what I wanted to accomplish here.

And finally, thank you to all the people who have watched and engaged with my videos. This is all for you, my beautiful visions, who in my darkest hours extended a tremendous support that has literally saved my life.

—JV

Printed in Great Britain
by Amazon